THE PLAYFUL WANTON

MERRY FARMER

THE PLAYFUL WANTON

Copyright ©2019 by Merry Farmer

Cover design by Erin Dameron-Hill (the miracle-worker)

Paperback ISBN: 9781687478078

Click here for a complete list of other works by Merry Farmer.

If you'd like to be the first to learn about when the next books in the series come out and more, please sign up for my newsletter here: http://eepurl.com/RQ-KX

 Created with Vellum

For the REAL Playful Wonton

(my friend Julie's cat ;))

CHAPTER 1

SHROPSHIRE – SUMMER, 1816

*A*dolphus Gibbon, Bow Street runner, had a reputation for patience and persistence. He always caught his man in the end. But as he stood by one of the tall windows in one of what seemed like an infinite number of parlors at Hadnall Heath, the country home of Lord Rufus Herrington, staring out at the rain-soaked garden and thick, grey clouds, he bristled with edginess.

His investigation was taking too long. Too long by far. Predominantly because the man he was hunting, a wealthy, young buck by the name of Henry Ward, hadn't even arrived yet. The ridiculous house party had been going on for more than a week. Rufus had promised Ward would be there. Adolphus had dragged the barmaid, Ivy Percy, out to the countryside from London so that she could identify Ward when the blighter showed up. It was cruel to wrench the woman away from her employment and her family for so long. It was cruel for him to lead the female party guests along by pretending he was there to find a mate. And it was cruel for him to have to idle away countless days doing something as frivolous as pretending to have fun.

"We've done everything we can," Rufus said, entering the room with a jolly smile.

Adolphus turned sharply to him, clasping his hands behind his back. "I beg your pardon?" he asked in his deep, sonorous voice.

Rufus continued to grin as he crossed the room and took up a position at the window beside Adolphus. He let out a dramatic sigh and nodded to the rainy landscape stretching away from the house. "We've prayed to Thor, the thunder god. We've pleaded with the heavens to stop raining. I'm reasonably certain a few virgins have been sacrificed since the party began." He paused, his grin turning cheeky. "Well, I'm certain virginity has been sacrificed, at least."

Heat flooded Adolphus's face and he snapped to stare out the window once more. The Herrington's house party was little more than a celebration of debauchery, as far as he was concerned. He supposed the scores of young people who had ventured so far from London to seek mates felt they were out of the eye of the *ton*, and therefore that they had license for all manner of lascivious behavior. Indeed, one marriage had taken place already, if the shocking behavior and sudden flight of Lord Sullivan Whitlock and Miss Felicity Murdoch to Gretna Green could be considered a marriage. Adolphus had his suspicions about several other couples besides them.

Rufus chuckled as though he could read Adolphus's thoughts. "Don't look so priggish, Gibbon," he said. "House parties are made for indiscretion. That's how half the marriages of the *ton* are made."

"No doubt," Adolphus muttered.

It wasn't that he disapproved of amorous adventures. He had been raised on the fringes of the aristocracy in London, not among the prudish middle classes of the countryside. He knew that far more transpired between virile young men and women behind closed doors than was ever spoken about in public. That was part of the problem. It had been close to two years since he'd felt the warmth of a woman's body tangled with his. Two years since he'd had anything but his trusty right hand to find release. He liked to think of himself as a man of stoic restraint, but if he were honest with himself, being in a country house filled with men and women in a constant state of flirtation and arousal had wreaked havoc on his senses.

In short, he was desperate for it. Him, an upright citizen and respected Bow Street Runner. He wanted it so badly that he was on the verge of taking to wearing unfashionably long coats to hide the evidence. And he owed the entirety of his sorry state to—

A rich peal of laughter preceded Lady Eliza Towers's appearance in the doorway. She skittered to a stop and her friend, Lady Ophelia Binghamton, careened into her. The two young ladies giggled as they righted themselves, then stepped more sedately into the room.

"Forgive the intrusion," Lady Eliza said, her expression seeming to take on a sultry quality as she gazed at Adolphus. "We are searching for something. Please continue with your conversation and disregard our presence."

Rufus laughed and nodded. "Consider yourselves ignored." He turned back to Adolphus.

Adolphus's attention refused to leave Lady Eliza. She was everything he'd always desired in a woman. Her blonde hair was a crown of gold atop her head, delicate tendrils curling down to brush her slender neck. Her gown did little to hide her lithe shape. Her legs must have been long under its soft folds. And her breasts…. His heart skipped a beat and blood pumped straight to his cock at the sight of them, straining up against her neckline in their fullness. The way she dashed about the room, whispering to Lady Ophelia as they shifted books aside on the shelves, checked behind the curtains, and handled every ornament on the mantle, showed her form off to perfection.

What he couldn't do to that form! He instantly imagined her draped across the settee that stood between the two of them as she continued her search. He could see one of her long legs hiked over the back of the seat, the other sliding off the front, her glistening cunny exposed. He fantasized about her breasts heaving, her nipples hard, as she panted, open-mouthed, desperate to be fucked. He could practically feel how tight she would be as he pounded into her, balls-deep, and how she would scream his name when he made her come. He would spend himself so hard—

Rufus cleared his throat, dragging Adolphus out of his shameful thoughts and back into the cold, dreary present. The man wore a grin that told Adolphus he knew exactly what had been on his mind.

"You're in luck," Rufus said with a devilish grin, lowering his voice. "My wife has a few entertainments in mind that might just get you what you want there."

"I'm certain I do not know of what you speak," Adolphus mumbled, glancing out the window with a frown.

"In fact," Rufus went on, ignoring him, "she should be announcing one of them any moment now."

Adolphus hummed, the sound matching the patter of the rain. He had to steer the conversation away from matrimonial games and the lust they produced. He had to think of something else than how delicious Lady Eliza's cunny would taste as he made her come.

"Is Miss Ivy safe?" he asked, frowning. Business. That was the only thing that would take his mind off the almost painful urge that gripped him.

Rufus let out a breath and shook his head, slapping Adolphus's back. "She's as safe and comfortable as could be expected," he said. "My staff are taking very good care of her. She's even offered to help out in the kitchen as a way to repay the kindness being shown to her."

"I don't know if I would call it kindness," Adolphus said, turning to Rufus and risking spotting Lady Eliza out of the corner of his eye as he did. "She is the primary witness to Ward's crime, but I do not rest easy, knowing I've removed her from her life with the sole purpose of providing identification."

"Plenty of others saw Ward trample that man to death that night," Rufus said, his expression sobering. "You'll have half a dozen witnesses and more identifying him once this goes to court. Bob Norris was well-liked. Ward was a blackguard of the highest order for running him down with that vicious horse of his, then leaving the scene of the crime."

"Miss Ivy served him in the pub," Adolphus reasoned. "She can not only identify him, she can attest to how much he had imbibed that night and the substance of his argument with Norris."

"If you say so." Rufus sent him a reassuring smile. "In the meantime, you're at a party whose expressed purpose is to make couples. You're past the age when you should marry, you come from a respectable family, and you're settled in the world." He glanced subtly toward Lady Eliza, then leaned closer to whisper, "Take a wife, man. Anyone with eyes can tell that you need one."

Adolphus stiffened, tilting his chin up in offense. He would have demanded what Rufus meant by a comment like that, but the infuriating man stepped away, winked, then crossed the room to the ladies.

"Lady Ophelia," he said, looking as though he were about to tell a joke. "I understand you are attempting to solve the mystery of a certain key you discovered in the orangery?"

Lady Ophelia seemed surprised. "I am, my lord."

"I may have a few suggestions for you," Rufus said, touching the small of her back and leading her out of the room.

Lady Ophelia glanced anxiously over her shoulder at Lady Eliza as Rufus rushed her from the room. She peeked at Adolphus as well, which seemed to settle in her mind why Rufus was removing her from Lady Eliza. As they turned the corner, she sent Lady Eliza an encouraging look.

Adolphus would have groaned in torment, but he needed all of his powers of concentration at that moment. He was alone in a room with Lady Eliza Towers, and in spite of his most valiant efforts, he could not tame the lust that threatened to undo him.

ELIZA COULDN'T BELIEVE HER LUCK. STUMBLING across Adolphus Gibbon while attempting to find whatever Ophelia's key unlocked was a gift from the gods. She would have to say a special prayer to Aphrodite and Eros that evening before going to bed. And bless Rufus

Herrington as well. She couldn't have arranged a more agreeable meeting if she'd tried.

"This is a treat," she said, lowering her head slightly so that she could glance up at Adolphus with a coy smile as she stepped slowly closer to him. "Although I'm certain my chaperone, Mrs. Lakes, would have a thing or two to say about a young lady being alone in a room with an eligible bachelor."

"I'm not—" Adolphus started, but stopped and let out a sharp breath. "We should not risk the impropriety of being caught alone, unchaperoned," he said shortly. "I dare not risk your reputation in such a way."

Eliza laughed. He truly was sweet under all that stiffness. And if she wasn't mistaken, she noted a particular kind of stiffness that left her heart racing and her mouth watering. "I believe the usual rules of propriety have been thoroughly abandoned at this particular party," she said. "In fact, I would not be surprised if polite society whispers about the horrors and immorality of this party for years to come."

She arched one eyebrow alluringly, stepping ever closer, hoping he would feel her invitation to sin. She'd long since stopped worrying about her own reputation, after all. Attending Mrs. Dobson's School had been a sign to the *ton* and any person of respectability that she was fallen. Even without that, the rumors that a certain friend of her brother had spread ever since his visit to her family's home three years ago had damaged any chance she might ever have of being seen as anything other than a wanton. Nothing she could say or do to Adolphus Gibbon could sink her any lower in the *ton's* eyes.

Adolphus cleared his throat and shifted uncomfortably. "Yes, well," he said, seeming as though he didn't know what to say.

Eliza reached the window where he stood and paused, studying him with a look of frank appraisal. He truly was a handsome man—tall, with broad shoulders, a strong jaw, and eyes that seemed perpetually narrowed in thought. Now that she stood close to him, she could see those eyes were blue. And he smelled lovely as well, like lemons with a hint of musk.

"How does it feel to attend a party that is likely to be seen as notorious?" she asked, smiling.

He cleared his throat again. "I doubt it will affect me, seeing as—" He paused and a strange look flashed into his eyes. He continued with, "Seeing as I do not socialize in the sort of circles that would find a salacious house party any reason for concern."

Eliza stood a bit straighter, keen interest zipping through her. "What circles do you socialize in?" she asked, genuinely interested in the answer.

"I...." He paused, pressed his lips together, then tried again. "I do not have time for calls or leisure. My employment as a Runner prevents me from engaging in most frivolous activities."

Eliza blinked. "But surely you must take time to enjoy yourself now and then. Even the most important employment allows a man time to himself. What do you do in your free time?" She inched closer to him, reaching out to touch one of the buttons on his coat.

He flinched and pulled away slightly, but Eliza could have sworn the bulge in his breeches increased.

"I read," he said in a tight voice. "And I walk."

"At the same time?" She glanced up at him with a teasing grin.

"No," he answered without elaborating.

She pushed on with, "And do you have company while walking? Perhaps a particular female friend?" She batted her eyelashes.

"No," he answered, even curter than before, his face reddening.

She made a tsking sound and resumed playing with the button on his coat. "It's always better to go walking with amiable company."

"I am surprised to hear you say so, Lady Eliza."

Eliza blinked in genuine surprise and swayed back to look at him. "How so?"

"Are you not a noblewoman's daughter?"

"I fail to see how that informs my belief that handsome men of quality should have female companionship," she answered.

He turned a deeper shade of red. "While I am flattered by your concern and attention, I am equally baffled by it. I have no position in society and only a modest income. Should you not focus your attentions elsewhere?"

Eliza couldn't help but laugh, though she prayed he

wouldn't think she was laughing at him. At least not derisively. "My dear Mr. Gibbon, it does not signify what my status in the aristocracy is. No woman of questionable morals is worthy of the company she seeks." She was surprised at how bitter her words sounded.

She was even more surprised by the softness that came to Adolphus's eyes. "I fail to see how anyone could accuse you of questionable morality."

Her lips twitched into a wry grin. "We first met while I was attending Miss Dobson's School, Mr. Gibbon. You know what sort of an institution that was."

"It was a reformatory," he said, his shoulders loosening somewhat.

"And as for showering my attentions on men of status and title...." She shrugged. "I have no need to marry for position, even if I could. My dear uncle settled a considerable fortune on me, to be paid out at the time of my marriage. He did not specify a particular social class for my future groom."

She delivered the information with a blatantly suggestive grin, hoping Adolphus could see it as the invitation it was.

"I...." he stammered.

"I have admired you since the investigation into the disappearance of the Chandramukhi Diamond," Eliza rushed on. "The way you took command of that operation and worked so diligently to bring the thieves to justice was...." She finished with a restless, shivering breath, biting her lip.

"Your admiration is appreciated," he said, sounding uncertain.

"And I was so pleased when I discovered you'd been invited to this party," she went on. Her blood was racing, her body thrummed with excitement, and if she wasn't mistaken, the air between her and Adolphus crackled with sexual tension. She found herself wanting to peel his clothes off and ride him until they were both raw and undone. "I have wanted to know you much better for some time now," she continued, toying with his button until she slipped it through its loop and loosened his coat. "But do you know what I want even more than that?"

"Dare I ask?" His voice was rough with lust.

Eliza grinned in triumph, aching in all the best places. "Do you know what I want from you so intensely I can taste it?" she whispered.

"I could not imagine." He leaned closer to her. She could feel the heat of his body, smell the salt of his skin.

"I want...." She swayed close, lifting to her toes. "I want...."

"Yes?" he growled.

She brought her mouth to within inches of his. "I want to make you laugh, Mr. Gibbon."

He was stock still for a moment, his eyes wide with incredulity, his body practically vibrating with tension. Then he let out a long breath on a wordless syllable that proved beyond a shadow of a doubt that she had him wrapped around her finger.

"Do you wish to laugh with me, Mr. Gibbon?" she asked in a whisper, staring at his open lips.

"I—" His hands lifted to brush her waist.

"There you are."

Caro's loud greeting from the doorway startled Eliza. She leapt back from Adolphus, realizing too late that her aims would likely have been better served if her friend had seen her wrapped intimately around him. Then, perhaps, the two of them would be forced to marry to avoid scandal. Although considering all that she'd only just said about the reputation of the party, it wouldn't have been enough.

Adolphus had stepped back as well. He did more than that, he walked away from Eliza, standing near the settee in a way that Eliza was certain was intended to block the sight of his arousal from Caro's prying, teasing eyes.

"You must come to the grand parlor at once," Caro said. "I am about to make an important announcement about a game we shall all delight in playing. Come, come."

She gestured toward Eliza and Adolphus, then hurried on.

Eliza turned to Adolphus with a pleasant smile, as though nothing untoward had happened or was about to happen. "Shall we, Mr. Gibbon?" She held a hand out toward him, hinting he should offer his arm and escort her to the grand parlor.

Adolphus cleared his throat, tugged at the hem of his

coat, then seemed to force himself into some semblance of propriety. "As you wish, Lady Eliza."

Eliza smiled as he stepped forward, slipping her hand into the crook of her arm. "I wish a great many things, Mr. Gibbon," she whispered as they headed out of the room.

And if she wasn't mistaken, she was well on her way to getting them.

CHAPTER 2

*B*loody sodding hell. Adolphus cursed himself in the strongest words he could think of as he escorted Lady Eliza out of the parlor and down the winding halls toward the grand parlor. Slowly. Not because he wanted to linger by her side in a bid to spend more time with her, but because he needed the extra seconds to will his cock into submission. He was at Hadnall Heath on business, to catch a killer, not to display the size of his manhood to all and sundry who glanced his way at an inopportune moment.

"You seem tense, Mr. Gibbon," Lady Eliza said in that teasing voice of hers that did nothing to improve his state of arousal. "Are you well?"

"Quite well, my lady," he mumbled, fighting to ignore all the impulses raging within him that made those words a lie.

She leaned closer to him, resting her free hand on his arm. "It's only that I fear I make you nervous."

"Not at all," he lied. "I am merely...." He couldn't come up with an excuse quickly enough. They neared the grand parlor and the din of dozens of party guests chattering in anticipation. He grasped hold of that feeble thread and said, "I am merely reticent when it comes to crowds."

Her brow lifted in surprise and her eyes sparkled. "What a curious admission. I have never minded crowds myself. Particularly if I can be the center of attention."

They stepped through the doorway into the grand parlor at that moment, and Adolphus turned his head to study her. Yes, he could see how she would enjoy being the center of attention. But in his observations of the workings of the party so far, he had never seen her command the spotlight. Not like Lady Malvis Cunningham or Lady Philomena Montgomery. Those ladies had half the gentlemen of the house party clamoring for their attention. Lady Malvis in particular seemed to jealously demand attention. Perhaps because of the humiliation her father had received the week before at the hands of Miss Murdoch. But in spite of Lady Eliza's words, she had largely been ignored by the bulk of the guests.

It wasn't until that moment that he stopped to think how strange and how wrong that was. If it were up to him, every eligible lordling in the county would be throwing roses at her feet and begging for kisses.

A stab of jealousy hit him at the thought. On second thought, perhaps not.

Lady Eliza laughed unexpectedly. "Mr. Gibbon, you are a fascinating specimen of masculinity," she said.

"I beg your pardon?" he mumbled as they found a spot to the side of the gathering of party guests.

Lady Caroline cut through the assembly to make her way to the front of the room, where Rufus was holding a large basket that appeared to be filled with slips of paper.

"You are aware that you blush deliciously when thoughts are flying through your handsome head, are you not?" Lady Eliza asked.

Being made aware of the fact sent more heat to Adolphus's face. Perfect. Heat in his face and his groin. He would never live the ridiculous house party down. "I was not aware," he mumbled.

He was saved having to say more as Lady Caroline raised her voice and called, "Ladies and gentlemen, if I could have your attention, please."

Adolphus cleared his throat and straightened in a show of focus. The stiff posture did nothing to hide his state of arousal, but at least the men and women that surrounded him and Lady Eliza seemed far more interested in what Lady Caroline was about to say than in judging him.

"I'm so excited," Lady Eliza said, gripping his arm tighter. "I wonder what sort of mischief Caro is about to spring on us all?"

The answer came immediately.

"My dear friends," Lady Caroline began. "Since the weather has refused to cooperate with our recreational plans this summer—"

"It's been a damn nuisance," Rufus added, rolling his eyes at the rain-streaked windows.

Lady Caroline sent him a teasing, scolding look before going on. "Since all of my plans for outdoor activities to keep you entertained have been thwarted, my darling husband and I have come up with an indoor activity of astounding scope to keep you diverted in the happiest possible way."

A murmur of anticipation passed through the assembly. Lady Eliza smiled as though she were about to be handed a prize. Adolphus's heart leapt in his chest as he stole a peek at her. Instantly, he reprimanded himself for such frivolous emotions. He scanned the guests, telling himself that the nobility was as ridiculous as children when it came to keeping themselves entertained. But that did little to quell the way his pulse kicked up as Lady Caroline went on.

"I have arranged for you all to unravel a mystery."

"Ooh, lovely," Lady Eliza whispered. "You should be quite adept at this," she told him, hugging his arm tighter.

It was beautiful torture. He burned so hot for her he thought he might melt.

Lady Caroline went on, gesturing to the basket Rufus held. "In this basket are a variety of riddles, clues, if you will, that will lead you on to more clues. As you decipher each one, you will come closer and closer to a prize.

There is only one prize, which is hidden in a specific location, but each of these clues represents many paths to reach that prize."

"Give us the clues, then," one of the livelier young bucks at the party called out. His fellows and many others laughed at his outburst.

"Ah, but I will," Lady Caroline answered him. "Just as soon as I explain the rest of the rules." There was a moment of laughter before she continued with, "All of you, my guests, will be paired up into couples to follow the clues and hunt for the prize."

A murmur of excitement passed through the assembly before another brash young gentleman called out, "I choose Lady Philomena to be my partner."

His declaration was instantly met by protest from the other men who had been vying for Lady Philomena's attention. Lady Caroline tried to speak up to stop the riot, but in the end, Rufus had to whistle loud enough to break glass to get the row to stop.

"The couples will be chosen at random," Lady Caroline announced. "We have a second basket with each guest's name written on a slip of paper. We will choose partnerships in this way."

A burst of disappointment filled Adolphus. The odds of him being paired with Lady Eliza were small. Hard on the heels of that thought, he cursed himself all over again for being a fool.

"Lady Ophelia, if you would help me choose the

partnerships," Lady Caroline went on, calling Lady Eliza's dear friend out of the crowd.

Lady Ophelia looked confused, but she made her way up to the front of the room, where Rufus exchanged his basket of clues for what Adolphus presumed were the names. Lady Caroline gestured for Lady Ophelia to come close. She leaned in and whispered something in Lady Ophelia's ear. Even across the room, Adolphus could sense foul play. That thought seemed to be confirmed by the sudden switch from bafflement to mischievousness in Lady Ophelia's expression.

Lady Ophelia reached into the basket and withdrew two slips of paper. Her grin widened, and she called out, "Count Fabian Camoni and Lady Alice Marlowe."

A ripple of curiosity passed through the room as the guests twisted and turned to find the two people in question. Count Camoni looked decidedly pleased, while Lady Alice looked intimidated. Her father, on the other hand, couldn't have looked happier.

"Lord George Allenby and Lady Philomena Montgomery." Lady Ophelia announced the second couple, causing a firestorm of gloating from Lord Allenby and protests from his rivals.

Their noise quieted as Lady Ophelia continued, selecting couples from the basket. Adolphus's suspicions mounted with each new couple that was announced. Some of them did, indeed, seem random, but the majority of the pairings fell in line surprisingly well with several of the couples he had observed making each other's acquaintance in particular ways since the start of the party.

His suspicions were proven to be well founded when Lady Ophelia fished two more slips of paper from the basket, grinned from ear to ear at Lady Eliza, and announced, "Mr. Adolphus Gibbon and Lady Eliza Towers."

Twin jolts of dread and delight stiffened Adolphus. Forget his face, he felt his whole body flush with heat, especially when Eliza hugged his arm and jumped up and down in a way that brushed her tantalizing breasts against him.

"This is brilliant," she said with a giggle. "We shall win the prize, I'm certain."

Adolphus shifted to study her, wondering if she had anything to do with their entirely non-random coupling. But there was too much delight in her expression, too much surprise. Whatever Lady Caroline was up to, Lady Eliza wasn't a part of it.

Lady Eliza was beautiful when she was in a playful mood, however. A light sparkled in her blue eyes. The pink of her cheeks was beyond kissable. Her smile could light a thousand candles at a glance. She was everything that he had been missing from his life for so long. God, but he couldn't decide whether he wanted to recline at her feet and listen to her recite sonnets or fuck her until she cried out his name. He wanted both.

The selection of the couples finished while he was in

the middle of his daydreams and the room erupted into activity as the chosen pairs sought each other out.

"We will be triumphant." Lady Eliza repeated her earlier sentiment. "I know we will. I do not see how we could fail to win the prize."

The only prize Adolphus cared about was her.

No, he scolded himself as soon as the sentimental thought settled over him. He was there to work, not to fall in love.

"Now that you have found your partners," Lady Caroline went on, sparing him the torture of examining his conflicting thoughts, "I must warn you about one further element of this hunt."

The noise of the couples died down a bit as they all turned to listen to her.

"Beware the Trickster," she said with so much mischief that it should have been illegal. "The Trickster will be circulating amongst you all, attempting to thwart your efforts to solve the clues and going out of his way to throw up impediments to your progress."

"Such as?" Lady Malvis demanded with a frown.

Lady Caroline's grin grew. "You shall simply have to wait and see. Now, please come forward to retrieve your first clue."

She went on to remind everyone that each clue would take each couple on a different path, even though they all lead to the same prize, but no one was listening to her. They crowded around Rufus, pushing and elbowing each other, as if they could select a clue that was better than the rest.

"Come on," Lady Eliza said, grabbing his hand and tugging him forward. "We don't want to let the others get ahead of us."

She was charming as well as sultry. It wasn't the thought he expected to have as she dragged him out of the relative safety of the corner of the room and into the thick of the crowd. The couples that had already received their first clue were spreading out to read them while the rest continued to cluster around Rufus. Lady Eliza navigated through them all like a ship's captain expertly navigating shoals. He would have bumped into every person and spent an age muttering embarrassed apologies to them all, but a path cleared for Eliza. It was mesmerizing.

"We're here for our clue," she announced when they made it to Rufus.

"Pick away," Rufus said, holding out the basket for her. As Eliza picked, Rufus winked conspiratorially at Adolphus.

"You didn't have anything to do with this, did you?" he asked, nodding slightly to Eliza.

"Of course not," Rufus said with a broad grin. "It was entirely random, man. You should know that."

Adolphus hummed, unconvinced. "I do not have time for silliness and games," he muttered to Rufus as Eliza distracted herself with the basket of clues. "You say Ward is arriving soon. And I should be looking out for Miss Ivy."

"She's fine," Rufus said. "Life cannot be all work. Sometimes you have to play."

Between the way Rufus nodded to Eliza and the teasing in his tone, a knot of foreboding formed in Adolphus's stomach. There was more to the hunt than Rufus or Lady Caroline was letting on, yet he felt helpless to do anything about it.

"Here we go," Eliza said, stepping away from Rufus and the basket with a folded slip of paper in her hand. "Now to solve the riddle."

She grabbed Adolphus's hand once more and dashed back to the side of the room, where they could have a modicum of privacy. Once again, the shuffling, excited couples cleared a way for her, though on second thought, Adolphus wasn't certain if it was because Eliza had power, or if the others were trying to avoid her.

By the time they reached their old spot, it didn't matter.

"Now for the clue," Eliza announced, huddling close to him and opening the slip of paper. *"You will find me where trees flourish and woodland creatures frolic. I am the wisest of them all."*

Adolphus frowned, a more comfortable part of his mind grinding into motion. "Trees and woodland creatures," he said, thinking aloud.

"It cannot be outside," Eliza said. "Not with this weather."

The gears turned, and inspiration struck. "Is there a

room in the house that is decorated like a forest?" he asked.

Eliza brightened. "There is. There's a parlor on the morning side of the house that looks just like a page out of some German fairy tale that takes place in the woods."

Adolphus nodded as though he'd discovered a key piece of information in a formal investigation. "That is where we should go."

Eliza took his hand and dashed out of the room. This time, he barely flinched at the touch of her hand or the way she pulled him along in her enthusiasm to search. Investigating was what he knew best. It was comfortable and soothing. Clues he could figure out far better than he could figure out lust or love or the tempting smiles that Eliza tossed over her shoulder at him as they jogged down the hall. And when had he started thinking of her by her given name instead the more proper "Lady Eliza" anyhow?

"I knew this was here," Eliza gasped, out of breath, as they reached a parlor at the far end of the east wing.

Sure enough, the room was decorated with a forest motif. Paintings of woodland scenes adorned the walls and small carvings of foxes, deer, and even an elf or two sat on the mantle and on the small tables interspersed between green-upholstered chairs and settees.

"Now all we need to do is find it," Eliza said.

Her chest heaved perfectly against the neckline of her gown, drawing Adolphus's full attention. He caught himself wondering if the fabric of her gown was simply textured or if the shape of her bodice was because her nipples were hard. They would certainly be hard once he suckled and teased them into points.

"Where do you think we should look?" she asked, turning to him with a glint in her eyes that said she could read his thoughts. In fact, her look was as much of an invitation as anything else.

Adolphus cleared his throat. "The wisest of forest creatures is an owl," he said, his voice rough.

"We should search for an owl, then," she said, swaying closer to him. "Although it has occurred to me that, once again, we are alone in a remote part of the house." She rested her hand against his thundering heart. "We could abandon the hunt and seek out another prize."

Her hand slid lower. There wasn't a doubt in his mind what she would end up fondling if she continued on her current course. He sucked in a breath, bracing himself, battling between pushing her away and letting her grab hold of him and—

A flurry of giggles preceded a second couple dashing into the room. Adolphus couldn't remember the names of the rosy-cheeked young people as they skittered to a stop at the sight of him and Eliza.

"Oh. We're terribly sorry," the woman said.

"Only, we believe our clue to be in this room," the gentleman followed.

Eliza peeled away from him, looking as though nothing even remotely out of the ordinary were going on. "Yes, our clue is in this room as well."

The gentleman frowned slightly. "It's not an oak, is it?"

Adolphus peeked down at himself. In fact, it was becoming entirely oak-like as they spoke.

"No, ours is an owl," Eliza giggled.

"How droll," the lady said, then set about searching the room.

As much of a relief as it was to be ignored while he was in a state, Adolphus had the feeling that his torment had only just begun.

"There's an owl over here," Eliza whispered, rushing to the mantle, where a majestic, stuffed owl resided.

Adolphus pulled himself together long enough to follow her. By the time he reached the fireplace, Eliza had already retrieved a folded slip of paper from under the base of the owl's stand.

"This is such fun," she said, her smile beaming, as she unfolded the second piece of paper and cuddled up to his side so they could read it together.

"I serve from dawn 'til dusk, a man of the foot. But at night, I lay my head here with a view of the stars."

"A footman's bedroom," Adolphus said, deciphering the clue instantly. "One with a window that looks out at the stars."

Eliza frowned, clearly caught up in the game. "But I'm certain all of the footmen's bedrooms look out at the stars. The servant's rooms are usually on the top floor."

"We found it," the other lady shouted from the opposite end of the room, waving the clue she'd discovered.

"Hurry," Eliza whispered, her expression bright with intensity. "We can't let anyone get ahead of us."

Adolphus nodded and took her hand, leading her from the room. "We'll have to search all of the rooms," he said, striding out to the hall and toward a door he thought led to the servants' stairs.

Two questions pricked at him as they ventured on. Why was he throwing so much energy into a manufactured mystery when he had real work in front of him? And why was he enjoying it so much?

CHAPTER 3

*E*liza could barely contain her giddiness as she raced up the servants' stairs with Adolphus half a step behind her. Solving a mystery was precisely what the man needed to take his mind off of his proper, stoic ways. He'd proven adept at solving clues, although she shouldn't have been surprised at that. And she wasn't ignorant enough not to see the temptation in his eyes as she held his hand while searching or stood close to him while reading the clues. Adolphus Gibbon was like dry tinder just waiting for a spark.

"I do hope Caro and Rufus's servants don't mind us rummaging about their rooms," she said, breathless from all the stairs they'd climbed, as they reached the top floor of the house.

Adolphus hardly seemed winded at all as they started down the narrow hallway lined with simple, closed doors. "This hall seems abandoned," he said.

"Oh?" She paused to turn back to him, trying to catch her breath. That was made harder as she watched him stride to one of the doors, his body fit and moving with feline agility, and open it.

He hummed as the door opened into a plain room with a simple bed, wardrobe, and washstand. Eliza crept up behind him, gripping his arm and craning her neck to look into the room at his side. All things considered, she felt awkward about invading someone else's private chamber. But as it turned out, Adolphus was right. Even though the room was fully furnished and the bed made, it was clearly unused. A thin layer of dust hung over everything.

"The next clue is not in this room," Adolphus declared.

Eliza blinked and rocked back. "What makes you so certain?"

Adolphus stepped back into the hall with a stern, businesslike look. He opened his mouth as if he were about to explain a case to an inferior but paused as his movements brought him flush with Eliza. She hadn't moved back fast enough, and he was forced to close his arms around her to keep her from falling over. She instantly reciprocated, leaning into him and gazing up into his startled face.

"I...er...that is...." he stammered, his gaze settling on her lips.

He shifted just enough to bring the firm spear of his erection into contact with her hip. Shivers of need shot through Eliza, turning her knees to jelly and her sex to a pool of liquid fire. He bent closer to her, his mouth coming ever closer to hers. She slipped one of her hands from his waist to his hip, then inched toward his backside.

He tensed as though she'd slapped him, which was the furthest thing from her mind, and flinched away from her. He cleared his throat and said, "The dust in the room is undisturbed. If your friends had left a clue in this room, they would have left footprints as well."

It took Eliza's hazy mind a moment to remember what he was talking about. "You're right," she said, unsurprised that the words came out in a breathless squeak. "We should keep searching."

She cursed herself as soon as those words left her lips, for they prompted him to remove his arms and step away from her. He cleared his throat again, tugged at the hem of his coat—which did nothing to hide the bulge in his breeches—and crossed to the door on the other side of the hall.

The heated moment passed, though Eliza was left buzzing with unspent need. Adolphus opened the door to another untouched room. Eliza skipped back to the end of the hall nearest the stairs and tried a few of the doors there. Within moments, she'd come to the same conclusion Adolphus had. The hall was unused. The servants currently employed at Hadnall Heath must have lived in another part of the house. But just as she found no signs of habitation, she spotted no signs that a clue was nearby either. At least, until—

"Eliza." Adolphus called her name from the last door on the hall. Her name on his lips, without a proper "Lady" attached to it, sent a renewed pulse of lust through her.

"Have you found it?" she asked, closing the door of the room she'd just peeked in and scurrying down the hall to him.

He didn't answer with words. Instead, when she reached his side, he pushed the door he was peering through open all the way. The room he'd been examining was larger than the others with slightly nicer furnishings. A large bed stood against one wall, covered with warm blankets and several pillows. An empty fireplace was nestled in the wall opposite the bed. The room contained the usual wardrobe and washstand, but what marked it as different from the other rooms was the placement of the windows. They did not look out horizontally over the landscape of Shropshire, they faced up, fixed into the slope of the roof over that section of the house.

"A view of the stars," Eliza said, repeating the clue they'd found in the parlor. "Yes, of course."

"And this room has clearly been occupied recently," Adolphus said, stepping cautiously into the room. "Or at least someone has been within the room."

"To place a clue." Eliza brightened, sliding past him to rush into the room. She reached the center of the room and turned in a circle. "I suppose this was designed to belong to one of the higher servants," she said, taking in every detail and looking for a slip of paper that would contain their next clue. "Perhaps the first footman or the butler."

"Perhaps," Adolphus said.

He sounded distracted, and when Eliza lowered her eyes from the curious window in the slanted ceiling, she caught him watching her. Watching her with pure lust. He was the picture of a man who wanted a woman, and it dawned on her that they were more than just alone, they were alone in a remote part of the house that was seldom visited.

"Oh, my," she said, pressing a hand to her chest—partially to still her heart and partially to draw his attention to her breasts, which felt particularly heavy at that moment. "Whatever shall we do next?"

She pictured him rushing toward her and sweeping her into his arms. Her imagination conjured pictures of him throwing her onto the bed, shoving her skirts up over her hips, unbuttoning his breeches, and taking her like a wild stallion took the mare he wanted. Her skin prickled with the need to be touched, and her sex throbbed in anticipation of being filled and stretched to its limit.

Instead of fulfilling her fantasy, Adolphus cleared his throat yet again, tugged at his collar, and turned to examine the room. "There are only so many places a clue could be hidden in a room of this size," he said in decidedly gruff tones.

Disappointment warred with Eliza's need to forge ahead, both with the clue and her attempts to seduce him. "If I were a clue, where would I hide?" she asked.

Eliza opened the wardrobe, but instead of clues she found two warm robes. Something about the sight of them stirred her amorous feelings even more than they'd already been stirred. Adolphus checked the fireplace but found nothing. They both steered clear of the bed at first, but Eliza's heart began to beat faster as she wondered if the inevitable use of a bed that cozy-looking was what Caro had had in mind all along. She wasn't fool enough to suppose that she had been paired with Adolphus randomly. From the moment the selection of couples began, Eliza had figured out Caro's game. Her friend was pushing couples together whom she thought should be together. It would have been just like Caro to throw her and Adolphus together, then to put them in a position where they could not resist temptation. There were advantages to having a clever strumpet for a friend.

"I cannot imagine where it could be," Adolphus said, coming away from the fireplace and eyeing the bed suspiciously. "I can only—"

"There it is!"

Eliza gasped as a bit of white caught her eye from the corner of the window. It was on the outside, peering in at them against the background of the gloomy sky. Adolphus spotted it as soon as she pointed it out, and the two of them rushed to the window.

"It should be simple to open the window and—"

The moment Adolphus unhooked the latch and pushed the window up, buckets-worth of water splashed in on them. Whether it was merely the accumulation of rain or whether the Trickster had sabotaged the window didn't matter. In seconds, both Eliza and Adolphus were soaked to the bone. The slip of paper flittered to the floor along with the water. Between gasping at the shock of so much cold water and the surprise of it all, Eliza managed to bend over to retrieve it. The paper had been dipped in wax—presumably after the clue had been written— preserving the writing.

But before she could read it, a peel of male laughter sounded from the hallway and the door to the room slammed shut. A moment later, the click of the lock rang through the room.

"Bloody hell," Adolphus grumbled, shutting the window and fastening the latch. The window was surprisingly watertight when closed. He strode over to the door and tried the handle. "Damnation," he growled. "It's locked."

"From the outside?" Eliza blinked and skittered to his side as fast as she could in her waterlogged dress.

Adolphus tested the handle again and rattled the door in answer to her question.

"Who would build a door in a way that would lock its inhabitants inside?" she asked, beginning to shiver.

"Perhaps we now know why the rooms on this hall are unused," Adolphus said, wiping water from his face.

"So we're locked in?" Eliza's shivering increased. She glanced at the clue in her hand. "I don't suppose this matters, then."

"What matters is finding the key and getting out of

here." Adolphus pushed away from the door and began a second search of the room. He moved stiffly, clearly uncomfortable in his soaked clothes.

As she watched him, a slow grin spread across Eliza's face. Caro was brilliant. She could not have manufactured a more enticing situation if she'd tried. Eliza's shivering was genuine, but the dangerous chill she felt on the outside was nothing to the heat that grew to towering levels within her.

"What if we cannot find the key?" she asked, stepping to the washstand and setting the clue aside. She hugged herself, giving free reign to her shivers and praying Adolphus would glance in her direction soon. "What if we are trapped here for days?"

"We will not be trapped here for days," Adolphus grumbled, going to the wardrobe and opening it. He frowned at the robes and felt his way along the upper shelf. "Rufus, you devil," he shouted at the door. "There is no time for this."

At last, he turned toward Eliza. She made certain to emphasize her trembling as he did. Instantly, his expression softened, and he marched toward her.

"You're cold," he said, rubbing his hands over her upper arms.

"One tends to become cold when she is doused with icy water and left in a room with no fire," she said, realizing the levels of Caro's genius as she did. Without a fire, there was only one way for her to warm up, one way to avoid the potential disaster a chill could cause.

Adolphus seemed to sense it too. He muttered something under his breath, twisting to study the room, likely looking for anything that could warm her up. His eyes settled on the bed, and he muttered an even stronger oath.

"What are we going to do?" she asked, knowing the answer full well.

He turned back to her, his eyes meeting hers and studying her with smoldering fire that looked as though it would burn through the last of his resistance. He swept his arms around her waist, tugging her so firmly against him that Eliza gasped in surprise, then bristled with need.

"Rufus is the devil," he growled, splaying a hand across her back and bending closer to her. "This is beyond bearing. I no longer have the power to resist. That bastard knew he could push me to my limits. Even if I wanted to—"

His fierce words dissolved into a moan of desire as Eliza cupped her hand around his erection and stroked him. He answered her bold move by slanting his mouth over hers and kissing her with such ravenous passion that it made her head spin. He parted her lips with his, thrusting his tongue into her mouth in imitation of what she hoped he would do much more of in short order. It was the most demanding kiss she had ever received, and she was helpless to resist him.

But he had only just begun. He yanked at the sodden ties holding her gown together, then tugged the soaked fabric over her shoulders, exposing them. His mouth followed, searing kisses across her neck and shoulders. He licked and nipped her skin as well, going so far as to suck hard enough to mark her as he did. His ferocity left her trembling from the inside out, as aroused by his unexpected passion as she was frightened by it. But it was the most delicious sort of fright she'd ever experienced.

"I want you," he breathed against her skin as he peeled her gown low enough to tug the laces of her stays. "I want you naked and wanton beneath me. I want your legs spread and your sex glistening with desire. I want you to take me deep and come hard as you scream my name."

Eliza could only sigh and squirm with restlessness at his demands. He yanked and pulled at her dress, shoving it down over her hips and practically tearing away her stays and chemise to get to her breasts. Once they were exposed, he cupped them possessively, raking his thumbs over her already taut nipples and sending bolts of sensation through her. He then bent close to her, capturing one breast in his mouth. He groaned in satisfaction as he suckled her, teasing her nipple with his tongue and teeth. It was his teeth in particular that sent ripples of pleasure through her. He was going to devour her whole.

That scintillating thought was blasted away to no thought at all as he shoved her gown over her hips, sending the whole messy thing to a wet pile on the floor, and cupped her sex suddenly and demandingly. It was such a bold, possessive move that she gasped. Never in the past had a man claimed her so quickly and decisively that way. His fingers reached to the heart of her, and he pushed two of them inside of her as he slammed his mouth over hers in another wild kiss.

Any illusion she'd had that she would dominate their lovemaking was shattered. He was going to take what he wanted from her in the most commanding way possible. That knowledge left her feeling too weak to stand and desperate to submit to him. Her sex throbbed as his fingers pressed deeper and as the heel of his hand ground against her clitoris. It was as terrifying as it was arousing to know he had her at his mercy and that he was about to do whatever he wanted to her.

"You want me to fuck you, don't you?" he whispered against her ear, inching her toward the bed. "You've wanted me balls-deep in your wet cunny since the moment we arrived at this party, haven't you?"

"Yes," she panted. "Oh, yes."

"You'll take it any way I give it to you, won't you?"

"Yes, please," she answered, almost pleading. Already, she felt as though she might explode from the inside out.

He maneuvered her toward the side of the bed, then spun her to face it and pushed her forward. She gasped as she caught herself on her arms, then arched so that her backside tilted up to him, knowing what he wanted. She was rewarded by the desperate sound of his breathing as he peeled off his clothes. As each wet piece hit the floor, the ache in her sex grew stronger and she inched her legs farther apart. Her arms shook as she heard the thump of his boots being thrown aside.

She dared to glance over her shoulder and was rewarded by the sight of him, naked and aroused, striding toward her. His body was as glorious as she'd imagined it would be, with broad shoulders, powerful arms and thighs, a tight abdomen with defined muscles, and a cock that left her whimpering in expectation. He was long and thick. His tip was flared and slick with moisture. He could pretend to be a stoic, serious man all he wanted, but the sight of his enormous erection standing up against a body hardened by physical activity proved that he was a man of flesh and blood and desire.

He was a man of needs as well, one who wasted no time. No sooner did she feel the warmth of his body flush against her backside than he grabbed hold of her hips and slammed deep into her. She cried out in shock and pleasure at how swiftly he took her, without tenderness or preamble. He was deep inside of her, stretching her almost to the point of pain, in an instant, and good Lord in heaven above, it felt delicious.

He gripped her hips so hard she was certain he would leave a mark as he jerked and pounded into her. She couldn't help but cry out desperately in time to his thrusts. She'd never had a man so large before, and the sensations were exquisite. The emotions that came with being taken so rapaciously by such a powerful man were so strong that she started to weep—not out of fear or sorrow, but because it was all just so overpoweringly plea-surable and wonderful.

Almost without warning, her body exploded into the most powerful and all-consuming orgasm she'd ever felt. It was made ten times more wonderful with him thick inside of her. She cried out with the pleasure, wanting to scream his name as he'd demanded, but too overcome to remember what it was. He surprised her once again as her waves of pleasure began to die out by jerking away from her, flipping her to her back, and tossing her fully onto the bed.

"I want to see your face when I come," he growled, climbing over her like a wolf stalking his prey. "I want to see how much you like it when I spill my seed inside of you."

His boldness took her breath away even more than his hands as he stroked her body, teasing her breasts. Fucking was one thing, as she'd learned too well once in her life already, but Adolphus's bold assertion that he was going to come inside of her with all the risks that entailed, was a declaration that no words of love could come close to matching. She found herself buzzing with pleasure all over again, a second orgasm whispering in readiness in the wake of the first one.

"I could feast on your body for an eternity," he whis-pered, bending closer to suckle one of her breasts. He took what he wanted from her savagely, filling her with arousal even as he dominated her beyond question. He left her breast all too soon and shifted so that he could devour her sex. "You like it," he said, an accusation and a promise.

She was helpless to resist him and far beyond the ability to speak as he wrenched her legs apart and buried his face in her sex. It was wildly arousing to find herself so close to unraveling so quickly after the first time. She felt like desire personified as he used his tongue and teeth to bring her right to the brink of orgasm a second time. When she crashed over the edge with a deep-throated cry and tremors of pleasure that made her lose her mind, he groaned in satisfaction.

"Wanton," he panted, shifting to bring his cock to her entrance once more. She caught a flash of devilishness in his eyes as he grinned and said, "I always liked wantons," and crashed into her once more.

The world of sensations his thick cock evoked as he mated with her in a different position was a revelation. True to his word, he watched her intently as he jerked into her, fast and hard. She whimpered with pleasure, submitting to him completely and crying out wordlessly in time to his thrusts. His face pinched harder and the tension radiating from him grew more and more intense with his thrusts until, at last, he let out an impassioned cry as his body shuddered and warmth filled her inside.

With that rush, the storm of tension broke. He let out a heavy breath and sagged, his full weight pressing down on her. He was a firm mass of muscle, but she loved the feeling of him covering her. Every drop of his energy was gone, so much so that he didn't pull out of her. That was perfect, as far as Eliza was concerned. She circled her arms and legs around him, holding him as though she would never let him go. He had been everything she could have hoped for and more.

Her thoughts were fuzzy and she could barely remember her own name, but she had just enough presence of mind to say, "I'm warm now."

CHAPTER 4

*G*uilt. Adolphus had never felt anything like it. It squeezed at his insides like a hundred vises clamped around every vital organ he possessed. It twisted and flayed him, making him feel like the worst sort of cad in existence.

And at the same time, he had never felt a sense of contentment that reached so deeply into his soul. Time had ceased to matter. He had no idea how long he'd been snuggled under the heavy blankets of the abandoned bed —which was exceptionally comfortable at that—Eliza nestled against his side. No, nestled wasn't the right word for it. She was wrapped around him like another blanket, their limbs tangled together, their skin touching everywhere. Her delicious breasts pressed against his chest and the soft heat of her sex warmed his hip.

He felt as men must have felt when their bodies had been blown to bits by cannon-fire—too disconnected to recover and too far gone to care. Above him, a harder rain had begun to drum against the upward-facing window, its rhythm soothing. He was tempted to go back to sleep. He was tempted to roll Eliza to her back and bury himself deep inside of her again. Even the thought of enjoying her eager sweetness again sent blood pounding to his cock. Possessing Eliza as he had was the single most satisfying sexual experience of his life. He wanted more. He wanted to see how far he could push her, how far they could push themselves, before the act became obscene. He wanted to vent every one of his unnatural urges with her and to have her moan with wanton need as he did.

Which, of course, only made his guilt flare hotter. What kind of animal would use a beautiful, high-born maiden as devilishly as he had? At least she hadn't been a virgin. It hadn't taken him long to determine that. But that didn't alleviate his guilt. Eliza deserved more than the beast he was. She deserved—

She sucked in a breath and stretched against him as she woke, banishing every one of his circular thoughts from his mind. When she let out her breath on a sultry, satisfied moan, his cock jumped in response. God help him, he wouldn't be able to function going forward unless he had her on a regular basis.

"Did that truly happen?" she asked in a sleep-hazed voice.

"I'm afraid it did," he answered, tensing.

She hummed happily, snuggling closer to him. "Good."

Her words hit him like a knife in his gut. "No, it was not good," he said, uncertain whether he should push away from her or stay where he was.

Eliza's eyes snapped open, and she lifted herself to frown down at him. "What do you mean it wasn't good? It was glorious and wild and satisfying."

"Yes, I mean, no. I mean, it was satisfying—" More so than he was prepared to admit to her. "—but it was ill-advised."

"Ill-advised?" She arched an eyebrow, looking rather like the strict governess he'd had when he was a boy.

"We are not married," he explained, sitting up and willing himself to face the situation logically, though logic was next to impossible with the bedcovers falling down to Eliza's hips, leaving her perfectly-formed breasts bared to him. He tried, and failed, not to stare at them as he went on with, "Though our marital state is something I intend to rectify immediately."

She blinked, making no move to cover herself. "I beg your pardon?"

At last, he dragged his eyes up to meet hers. "We will marry at once. We can have the banns read at your home parish or mine, whichever you'd prefer. Or we could travel up to Scotland with all haste, as your friend, Miss Murdoch, or rather, Lady Whitlock, did."

She continued to stare at him as though he'd sprouted antlers. "Is that your response to every woman you've bedded?" Clearly, she was offended.

"No," he answered, scrambling for an honest way to

46

express his feelings without making an ass of himself. "The majority of the women I've taken to bed in the past —and I should be clear that there have not been many— were of an ilk that did not require marriage as a rectification of the implications of the act."

God, he sounded like an ass even when he was trying not to. But he had no smooth words to describe the yearning in his gut at the sight of her, the hope that infused his soul at the idea of spending the rest of his life with her, and the joy that squeezed his heart, not to mention his cock, at the thought of having her beside him, in and out of bed, for the rest of their lives.

Still, she blinked at him, her mouth going slack in disbelief. "Are you proposing to me, Mr. Gibbon?" she asked, bristling with incredulity.

"Yes, of course," he said. "Our situation demands it."

She let out a humorless laugh, gaping at him. Then she shook her head. "No," she said. Any hope he had of understanding her answer was blasted away when she surged toward him, pushing him back against the pile of pillows at the head of the bed and straddling him. She brushed her hands up his chest and rocked her open hips against the stiffening length of his cock. "No, I won't marry you. Not if you propose like that."

He grabbed hold of her hips, unable to decide if he wanted to halt her movements or whether he wanted to thrust into her so she could ride him to another, shattering orgasm.

"I've dishonored you," he said, disturbed by how

rough his voice sounded and how close the animal within him was to breaking free. "You are a lady of worth and dignity. You deserve more than to be treated like a whore."

She paused, raising her eyes slowly to meet his. Her cheeks flushed pink, and an unreadable wealth of emotions filled her face. For a fleeting moment, he thought she would weep. The moment passed, though, and she continued rocking teasingly against him. "What if I am a whore?" she asked, her genuine emotion covered over with playfulness.

"You're not," he said, certain of it in a way he couldn't explain. All he knew was that there was more to Lady Eliza Towers than met the eye.

She stopped her seductive movements once more. This time, Adolphus sensed it was because something far deeper than lust had been opened within her. "I won't marry you," she said quietly, eyes downcast. "Not if you ask me like that."

"How shall I ask you, then?" He frowned, failing to understand why she didn't jump on the offer the way she appeared to want to jump on his erection.

She met his eyes, surprising him with the anger he saw there. "I want to be proposed to because you want me, not because you feel obligated or guilty."

Heat seared through him as she spoke aloud the shameful emotions he was feeling. "I do want you," he explained. "I would have thought that much was obvious." He flickered a quick glance down to his hard cock between them.

Once again, she surprised and confused him by pushing away from him and climbing out of bed. "Not like that," she said. "Though any woman of feeling would be ecstatic to have a man of your prowess in their bed for life."

He'd never had a compliment strike him with such embarrassment before. The pride of being told he was good in bed was nothing to his confusion at being rejected.

"Eliza, do be reasonable," he said, throwing back the covers and climbing out of bed himself.

As he did, the ping of something small and metal hitting the floor distracted him. Eliza turned back to the bed at the sound. She blinked, then hurried to the side of the bed and bent to pick up a key.

"Well," she said, her brow lifting. "I have a guess what this goes to."

She skipped over to the locked door, fitting the key in the lock. Adolphus tried not to be distracted by the sight of her breasts bouncing with her steps or the pink roundness of her bottom as she turned the key. There was a click, she tried the handle, and the door inched open.

"Why am I not surprised that the key was located deep within the bedclothes," she said, turning back to him, her wicked, mischievous grin returning.

Her gaze dropped to his body, or rather, his erection.

The shoots of pride he continued to feel were strangled by self-consciousness. Not that he had anything to worry about. He knew full well what he looked like and how appealing that was. His job demanded that he keep himself in top physical shape, and Nature had given him the sort of size that made women lose their minds. But if he continued to display himself while she stared at him as she did, licking her lips, they might never leave the bedroom. He crossed to the wardrobe, throwing it open and taking out one of the robes.

"Do you suspect this was all a deliberate ploy to get us into bed together?" he asked as he threw the robe around his shoulders. His clothes were far too wet still to dress in.

"Yes," she answered, her shoulders sagging in disappointment once he was covered. He felt the same disappointment when she retrieved a robe and hid her luscious body from him. "And I am eternally thankful to Caro for it."

"Thankful?" He sputtered. He frowned. He felt just as thankful as she said she was, though he wasn't about to admit it.

She shut the wardrobe door and turned to him with a coy smile. "I've never enjoyed myself more in all my life."

She was playing games with him, but he was determined to win. "Then accept my offer of marriage and I promise I'll fuck you just as thoroughly every night of our married life."

Using vulgar language was a gamble, but it seemed to pay off when her eyes lit with carnal fire. She drew in a breath that emphasized her every curve under the thick fabric of the robe. For a moment, he was certain she would cave in to him. Then she let out her breath, sagging.

"No," she said, marching toward the door. "I will not marry you unless you propose to me in a manner I find acceptable."

"In a manner you find...." He sputtered and snorted, dashed back to the bed to retrieve their hunt clue from the floor, where it'd fallen hours ago, then hurried after her. "Would you prefer I bring you flowers and prostrate myself in front of your friends?"

She stopped at the end of the hall, whipping back to him with a scowl. "I would prefer you propose because you want to marry me."

He gaped, throwing his arms out to his sides. "I do want to marry you. I wouldn't have proposed if I didn't."

She shook her head and continued on into the stairwell. "I shouldn't have expected a man to understand what I meant."

"Please explain," he said, storming after her.

"No," she said over her shoulder. "You wouldn't understand my explanation."

"You think not?" He was grateful that the servants' stairs were empty at that moment. As soon as they stepped out onto the hallway that connected the wings of the house, fear that they would be seen pummeled him.

"I know you wouldn't," she said. She clutched her robe more tightly around her and darted looks up and down the hall, evidently as concerned about being spotted as he was.

"We will speak about this later," he said, catching up to her side as though he would escort her to a ball. "For now, we need to retreat to our rooms to dress."

"My room is on that hall." She gestured across the very public landing they were about to cross to a hallway on the other side.

"So is mine," he grumbled, now seeing that his room's location wasn't an accident either. He was probably intended to sneak into her room for an assignation now and then. "Let's just hurry and—"

Everything stopped dead as they nearly ran into Rufus climbing the stairs. But it wasn't Rufus that startled Adolphus and turned his blood to liquid iron. It was the fact that Rufus was escorting Henry Ward up the stairs.

Of all the times to come face to face with the man he was trying to catch and bring to justice. Heat infused Adolphus's face as the four of them—he and Eliza, Rufus and Henry—met at the top of the stairs.

Rufus recovered from the shock first, bursting into a snort of laughter. "Look at the sight of you two," he said, an impish glow in his eyes. "Did you enjoy the search for your clue?"

Adolphus narrowed his eyes at the man, not so much because of the comment, but because Eliza suddenly seemed terrified and smaller than he'd ever seen her look.

"You don't happen to know anything about it, do you?" he growled.

"Not a thing," Rufus said, obviously lying.

Adolphus could have strangled him. Either Rufus was the Trickster or the Trickster was operating on Rufus's orders. But far more than the way his host seemed to be laughing at his expense, Adolphus's ire was raised by the way Ward grinned at Eliza.

"Well, well, Lady Eliza," Ward said. "We meet again."

"Mr. Ward," Eliza said, clutching her robe so tightly around her that Adolphus worried she would strangle herself.

"And how is your brother?" Ward asked.

Adolphus was inclined to pummel the man for attempting to hold a conversation with a lady of refinement when she was clearly in a state of distress, not to mention undress.

"He is well, sir," Eliza answered, meeting Ward's eyes with a sort of boldness and defiance that made the hair on the back of Adolphus's neck stand up. "Edmund and my parents are touring Italy at present."

"Yes, well, I suppose they'd have to after the way your father's debts were called in last winter, eh?" Ward winked at her.

Adolphus saw red. It was outrageous for the man to speak of the difficulties Eliza's family was undergoing, but to wink at her? More than ever, he wanted to bring the full weight of the law down on the man's head.

"If you will excuse me," Eliza said, nodding to Ward, then sending Adolphus a frustrated look. "As you can see, I find myself in a state inappropriate for company after being doused with rainwater while in search of a clue. I must retire to my room and change as soon as possible."

She turned and dashed off before any of them could say a word of encouragement or goodbye.

"I see the Trickster fooled you with his water trap, eh?" Rufus asked with a laugh.

"Quite," Adolphus grumbled.

"I'll have one of the footmen retrieve your clothes from the end room," Rufus went on. The fact that he knew or had guessed so much about what happened and where was further proof that he'd been directly involved.

"Your clothes?" Ward's brow shot up. That expression was followed by a grin so smug that Adolphus wanted to punch his teeth out. "Good Lord. I knew Lady Eliza was game, but I had expected she would mend her wanton ways after what happened to her family."

Adolphus wanted to kill the man, plain and simple. He wanted to run rough-shod over him the same way Ward had killed the dockworker by trampling him to death after a night in the pub. Because there was no doubt in his mind that Ward spoke from experience. The way he rubbed his mouth as he stared down the hall where Eliza had disappeared was unmistakable. That, coupled with the fear in Eliza's eyes, painted the very worst kind of picture in Adolphus's mind.

"I'm sorry, I don't believe we've met," Ward said a beat later, offering Adolphus a hand. "Henry Ward."

Adolphus would rather have untied his robe and exposed himself in front of the entire assembly of the house party than take Ward's filthy hand, but manners dictated he be civil. "Gibbon," he said in a low voice. "Adolphus Gibbon."

Ward's reaction was instantaneous. All color left his face. He let go of Adolphus's hand as though it were infected with plague and took a huge step back.

"Do you know, I've just remembered a pressing engagement that I really should attend to in London," Ward said to Rufus. "I'm sorry, old friend, but I really can't stay."

Rufus must have guessed what Adolphus figured out in an instant. Ward knew that he was being hunted. He knew the name of the man hunting him. He knew he was caught.

"Nonsense," Rufus laughed, doing an admirable job of pretending that nothing was wrong. "You've only just arrived. We're in the middle of a fantastic game that I know Caro would love to have you take part in."

Ward looked uncertain. He eyed Adolphus suspiciously.

"Besides," Rufus went on. "You've ridden such a long way and your horse has only just been put up for a rest. And the highwaymen this time of year are devilish. You couldn't possibly leave until tomorrow afternoon at the earliest. No, you couldn't leave until next Monday, I'm certain."

Adolphus attempted to send Rufus a look saying he'd crossed the line and laid it on too thick.

Ward continued to study Adolphus. "Gibbon, you say?" He cleared his throat. "The one associated with the Bow Street Runners?"

Before Adolphus was forced to admit the truth and frighten Ward away or lie, Rufus cut in with a sly, "You see why he's here, man." He raked Adolphus with a wry look. "Even a Runner needs to relax now and then."

"Maybe," Ward mumbled.

"Every man needs a bit of fun now and then, right Gibbon?" Rufus went on.

"Indeed," Adolphus grumbled. He hated the implication that he was toying with Eliza for sport even more than he hated the thought of losing his chance to nab Ward.

"So you see?" Rufus slapped Ward on the back. "I invited him to this party for the same reason I invited you. For fun. For enjoyment. For a little dip in the inkwell for those who need it. We're never going to live down the reputation of this party, so why not enjoy it?"

"I wouldn't mind reacquainting myself with Lady Eliza," Ward said, loosening up in a way that infuriated Adolphus. "She's enough to make any man think he's died and gone to heaven."

"Lady Eliza is otherwise spoken for," Adolphus said in deadly toned.

Ward had the good sense to look wary and inch farther away from him.

"There are plenty of biddable young maidens in attendance," Rufus went on, sliding an arm around Ward's shoulder and steering him toward a different hall than the one Eliza had retreated down. "I'll give you a complete catalog of the ones who are here to find husbands and the ones who are intent on enjoying themselves in other ways."

Adolphus stood where he was, watching the two men depart, with a deeply-etched scowl. Before they turned a corner, Rufus glanced back at him, a desperate look in his eyes, as if telling him they needed to act fast. He was right. The faster they brought Ward and Ivy face to face so that the young barmaid could identify Ward, the faster Adolphus could take him into custody. And if he had to use unnecessary force in questioning Ward, for Eliza's sake, he would have no qualms in doing it.

CHAPTER 5

*E*liza hurried along the hall to her bedroom, heart racing, clutching her robe tightly around her. The moment she reached her door, she shot through, shutting it behind her, then turning to lean against it, panting. What in the name of all that was holy was Henry Ward doing at Caro's house party?

It took her a few moments of resting her weight against the door as she gulped for breath, shivering as her body remembered the feeling of his touch and the way he dominated her. The sickening soup of emotions she'd felt all those years ago—fear, curiosity, horror, pleasure, and deep shame—swirled up in her once more. She'd been so certain she would never see Henry again.

At last, she gathered her courage enough to push away from the door and over to her washstand. She shed her robe and poured water from the pitcher into the basin, scrubbing herself as though she'd spent the afternoon with Henry instead of Adolphus. Scrubbing hadn't rid her of the disgusting feeling Henry had left her with years ago and it did little to make her feel better now. All she could do was dry off, dress, and put on the spritely smile she'd developed to hide the anxiety she'd never been able to scape from.

By the time she stepped back out into the hallway, dressed in one of her most conservative gowns with her hair pulled back from her face in the most unattractive style she could manage, the calm of resolve was beginning to take hold in her. Ophelia. She needed to find her friend and have a laugh. Ophelia was the rock she—and Felicity, for that matter—had clung to for the past two years. Without even knowing it, Ophelia's sweet presence and shy calm settled her. She needed her friend.

"Whatever are you doing in here alone?" she asked, trying not to sound as desperately relieved as she felt as she swept into the small library.

Ophelia stood by one of the shelves, reading a dusty old book. She gasped, then burst into a smile at the sight of Eliza. "I must confess, I became distracted in my search."

"And where is Mr. Khan?" Eliza asked. "You were partnered with him, were you not? Should he not be searching with you?" She crossed the room and threw her arms around Ophelia in a hug that was far tighter than it should have been.

When Eliza let go, Ophelia blinked rapidly at her, clearly startled. She replaced the book she'd been reading on the shelf with a confused look. That look dissolved into an airy laugh, and she said, "No, not the treasure hunt, the other search." She lifted the key she wore on a ribbon around her neck, the key she, Eliza, and Felicity had found the first day of the party but which they had yet to find the lock for.

"You are continuing that search when there is a far more interesting one afoot?" Eliza asked. She took Ophelia's hand and led her to one of the sofas in the room, sitting with her. It felt so wonderful to do something normal that the tension squeezing her began to fade.

Ophelia blushed, glancing down at her hands. "Mr. Khan and I spent most of the day searching for clues," she confessed.

"Why are you not still engaged in the hunt?" Eliza leaned her arm on the back of the sofa in an informal pose and scooted closer to her friend. "I am certain Mr. Khan was enjoying himself."

Ophelia blushed harder. "He is a kind and soft-spoken man," she said. "When he wants to be. Though I feel there is much he was holding back from me as we followed clues today. He was called away on business, an urgent message from his father, so we agreed to halt our efforts for the day."

"But what if someone else reaches the final prize before you do?" Eliza asked, realizing she and Adolphus were just as guilty of giving up the search for other activities.

Adolphus. Her heart squeezed at the very thought of

him. He wanted to marry her. At least, he had wanted to marry her before Henry Ward arrived on the scene. She was certain that Adolphus had seen the way Henry looked at her, seen the way she reacted. Adolphus was a Runner. His entire life was about noticing subtleties and interpreting clues. He would know in an instant what had been between her and Henry. He wouldn't want her anymore. He would cast her aside in disgust the same way her family and every other gentleman who had taken an interest in her had. Well, aside from the ones who changed their opinion of her and took advantage of her already ruined reputation.

"It appears as though the hunt has been paused for the day," Ophelia said, no outward indication that she could interpret Eliza's thoughts or that she knew she was thinking at all. "Caro hinted that there are a large number of clues in each path to the prize and that the entire game was designed to take days to play out."

"Of course," Eliza grinned, though she wasn't certain she felt that much mirth.

Ophelia's expression changed as she studied Eliza. "And why are you and Mr. Gibbon no longer searching?"

Eliza laughed, a trickle of delicious memories replacing the bad ones in her heart. "We were waylaid by the Trickster," she said, arching one eyebrow. "He trapped us in an abandoned servant's bedroom. He may even had been the one who rigged the window to douse us with water. We were forced to resort to extreme measures to warm up again."

"Yes, I have heard a great many reports of similar mischief by the Trickster," Ophelia went on, completely missing the sensual implication in Eliza's words. "I've heard of at least half a dozen couples who have been locked in rooms or trapped in wardrobes. I know of three couples who have given up the search entirely. Lady Malvis and her odious partner have declared the whole thing a stupid waste of time and have returned to preening and posing in the grand parlor instead of participating."

Eliza snorted. "She would do that."

Ophelia leaned closer, growing more animated as she went on. "A handful of couples have yet to emerge from their traps," she whispered. "Lady Lettuce Marlowe secretly told me that she heard sounds of an alarmingly scandalous nature coming from behind the door where one couple was trapped."

Eliza tried her best not to laugh. "Is that so?"

"It is. And one couple, Lady Philomena and Lord Allenby, have already announced their engagement."

"How delightful." Eliza smiled, knowing full well that it would have been two couples announcing their engagement, if only Adolphus had asked for her hand in a more meaningful way.

Of course, now that Henry had arrived, Eliza began to wonder if she should have accepted Adolphus's hand straight away. Would an engagement have protected her or would Adolphus have regretted tying himself to a woman of such low character?

"Lord Marlowe has been using the game to push his daughters toward horrible suitors," Ophelia went on. "Even though Caro was careful not to pair Lettuce with that Mr. Pigge, Lord Marlowe has insisted she and her partner complete the hunt with Mr. Pigge as a third, since his partner called off almost as soon as she saw who her partner was. And poor Imogen—"

Ophelia stopped in the middle of her gossip, her mouth open as she was startled by Henry's appearance in the doorway.

"Now this is a room I am happy to explore," Henry said, sauntering deeper into the room and approaching the sofa with a hungry smile.

Eliza's throat squeezed and her heart raced. She prayed to find the words she needed to tell the bastard to bugger off and leave her alone for a change, but her mouth went dry.

"Lady Eliza, you must introduce me to your charming friend," Henry went on, eyeing Ophelia the way a butcher eyed up a piece of meat.

"My friend was just leaving," Eliza said, standing so fast her head swam. She gestured for Ophelia to do the same.

"I...what...is there something...." Ophelia blinked at Eliza, her cheeks as pink as apples. She was clever enough to understand the hints Eliza was sending about whether she wanted to know Henry or not, though. She nodded, then started out of the room. "Do excuse me, sir," she said to Henry. As she reached the doorway, she sent Eliza one final, anxious look.

Eliza answered it with what she hoped was a reassuring smile. She thought Ophelia might change her mind and stay, but Henry turned to her with eyes narrowed, clearly telling her to get out without saying a word.

Ophelia left. Eliza swallowed and faced Henry, her smile gone. "What are you doing here?" she asked, dropping all pretense of amiability.

Henry stepped slowly around the sofa, laughing softly. "Come, Eliza. That's no way to greet an old friend, is it?"

"We are not friends," Eliza said, willing herself to stand her ground. She couldn't shy away from the memories of what she'd done years ago, so she had no right to shy away from facing them in the present.

Henry sent her a look as though he were indulging a temperamental child as he came to stand toe to toe with her. He lifted a hand and brushed her bare arm, making her wish she'd thought to wear a shawl or gloves or anything.

"I will not object if you wish to use another word for our acquaintance," he said, biting his lip as he watched the gooseflesh that appeared on her arm in the wake of his touch. He lowered his voice and went on with, "I still haven't forgotten how sweet and tight you were, or those beautiful sounds you made when I was balls deep in that slippery cunny of yours."

Eliza jerked away from him, feeling sick to her stomach. "I'm not the curious girl I once was," she said, barely audible.

Henry shrugged, stepping after her as she tried to inch away. "I overcame your objections easily enough that summer. There's no need to raise the same objections now."

"I didn't know any better." She was alarmed at how small and powerless she sounded, as if she had turned into the girl she'd once been all over again. "I didn't know enough to know how to tell you I was done with you."

"It wouldn't have mattered," he said. "I told you then and I'll repeat it now—I'm not done with you." He brushed the backs of his knuckles over her cheek. "What do you say we make use of this sofa to have a little tumble, eh? I'm half there already. All you'd have to do is bend over."

She wanted to slap him with everything she had in her. The only thing that stopped her was the sound of a man clearing his voice in the library's doorway.

Henry pivoted away from her, facing their intruder. As he moved out of the way, Eliza caught sight of Adolphus, his face like a thundercloud, glaring at her. Or perhaps just glaring at Henry. Either way, he looked angry enough to commit murder.

"Damn," Henry whispered, turning back to her. He'd lost a good deal of his color and all of the lasciviousness from his expression. "It's that Runner. I swear, he's after me."

Eliza swallowed, managing to find her voice enough to say, "Why would he be after you?"

The fear in Henry's eyes deepened, proving that he knew full well why, even if he didn't share the reason with Eliza. "I can't stay," he said, instantly turning and marching out of the room. He only glanced to Adolphus after he'd passed the man, right before disappearing around the corner.

Adolphus didn't seem to notice Henry's departure. He was too busy studying Eliza. The ferocity of his look made her feel undressed and unworthy. So much for all the beautiful things that had passed between them that afternoon.

"How do you know him?" Adolphus asked, crossing the room in a few, long strides to stand in front of her, like a judge about to pass sentence.

"What makes you think I know him?" It was foolish to play coy with Adolphus, but she was too frightened to stop herself.

Adolphus ignored her question. "Has he hurt you?"

Eliza blinked, slowly raising her eyes to meet his. Perhaps it wasn't fury and disgust she'd seen there after all. Perhaps it was possessiveness and concern. Whatever it was, she had no energy left in her to lie to him.

"He is a friend of my brother's," she said, unable to hold his intense gaze. "Five years ago, he spent the summer with my family. He seduced me, and then he continued to have me throughout the summer."

Adolphus was silent. It was unbearable. She peeked

up at him, only to find that his anger had doubled. She held her breath, waiting for him to curse her name and call her every manner of name he could think of—names she'd been called more than enough times before.

"Were you a willing party in this seduction?" he asked in a low growl that made the hair on the back of her neck stand up.

She opened her mouth to answer, as she'd answered the question too many times before. But unlike the times when she'd glibly confessed to curious gentlemen that she had been willing, that she'd enjoyed every moment, and that she was hungry for more, she hesitated.

"I don't know," she answered at last.

Adolphus's brow knit in confusion. "You don't know?"

He wasn't going to judge her. That tiny change in expression, the genuine puzzlement where she'd only ever received teasing and more illicit invitations, sparked hope within her.

"I don't know," she went on, facing him more fully and standing straighter. "I was seventeen. He was handsome. I was terrified of him. He trapped me in a situation I couldn't get out of. But then it felt good. I was confused and powerless to stop him." She glanced down. "I have no right to say he forced himself on me. He didn't. By the time we were done, I'd been a willing participant."

"He forced you," Adolphus growled.

She shook her head. "How could he have forced me if I let him do whatever he wanted? Not just that one time, but for the rest of the summer. I dreaded his knock on my door at night, but then I'd part my legs or get on my knees or do whatever he wanted. I liked it." She paused, glancing away. "And I didn't."

"He forced you," Adolphus said, louder and with more intensity.

"No one else thought so."

"I beg your pardon?"

She dragged her eyes back to him once more. "Every other man Henry whispered my filthy secret to didn't think he forced me. They didn't force themselves on me either." As much as it made her heart ache, she went on with, "You saw for yourself up there. I'm a slut. I'll never be anything else."

He moved to draw her into his arms so fast that it sent a wave of sharp fear through her, leaving her breathless.

"You are not a slut," he insisted in a low, threatening voice. "And I will murder Ward or anyone who says otherwise."

The emotions that hit her at his declaration were so strong that she laughed, even though it made no sense. "I should have told you how many men I've had before you," she said, aching with misery. "I should have given you the choice of whether you wanted to bed a whore."

"You are not a whore." He underscored his words by shaking her. The violence of his gesture should have frightened her, but instead, it seemed to loosen the cage she'd kept locked tight around herself. "You were used in the most despicable way possible. You were too young and innocent to know what was happening. Ward is a criminal, and I fully intend to bring him to justice."

Something clicked in Eliza's mind and she stared up at him. "You *are* here to investigate him, aren't you?"

Some of the tension drained from Adolphus's expression and body, though he continued to hold her. "He is guilty of trampling a man to death with his horse after a night of drunkenness at a pub in London. He left the scene, but I have brought a witness with me to identify him and bring him to justice."

A shiver of hatred for Henry passed through Eliza's heart. Trampling a man and leaving the scene was exactly the sort of thing Henry would do.

She was about to comment to that effect when Adolphus tightened his hands on her upper arms and said, "Marry me."

Eliza's jaw dropped. She gaped at him, unable to so much as catch her breath for a moment, let alone speak. After too long a silence, she finally managed, "No. You heard what I am."

"You are a delicate woman in need of protection," he said.

She was speechless all over again. No one had ever called her delicate in her life—not before Henry and certainly not after.

"I will protect you from the likes of Ward," Adolphus went on. "I will shield you from whatever villainous rumors he has spread about you. I will—"

"There you are."

They were interrupted as Rufus rushed into the room. He barely batted an eye at the proximity between Eliza and Adolphus, or at the intensity that made the air in the room crackle. He ignored all of it, marching straight up to Adolphus.

"Ward just tried to flee the house," he announced.

"He did?" Adolphus let go of Eliza and faced Rufus.

"Caro stopped him," Rufus went on. "She's talking up supper and getting him seated at the table as we speak. But we need to act fast."

"Where is Ivy?" Adolphus asked, marching past Rufus toward the door.

"Who is Ivy?" Eliza started after them.

"The barmaid from the pub," Adolphus explained. "The witness."

He didn't say more, but neither did he tell Eliza off when she followed him and Rufus down the hall and around a corner to an entrance to the servants' stairs. They hurried downstairs, passing various footmen and maids, who flattened themselves against the walls to make way for them, bowing and curtsying as they passed.

At last, they made it to a hallway off the kitchen that led past the scullery and a pantry to a remote, protected room.

Rufus stepped ahead of them and knocked on the door. "Hello? Miss Ivy?"

He was met with silence. Adolphus gestured for him to step aside, then took his place, knocking again. "Miss

Ivy, Ward is here. If you would kindly identify him, this can all be over and you may go home."

He too was met by silence. Eliza bit her lip, increasingly excited by the moment. At last, Adolphus reached for the door handle, pulling the door open.

The room on the other side was empty. A narrow bed and simple wardrobe were all that met them.

"Where is she?" Rufus asked.

"Miss Ivy?" a middle-aged woman, the cook, asked from the hall behind them. When all three of them turned toward her, she shrugged and said, "She's gone."

CHAPTER 6

*I*t was because the house party had already wreaked havoc on his emotions, robbing him of the ability to keep himself in check. That was why Adolphus turned to the cook with every fiber of his being bristling with anger and alarm and bellowed, "She's what?"

The poor cook stumbled back with a terrified groan, clutching a hand to her heart, losing all color, and stammering instead of giving an answer.

"Steady on, man," Rufus told him in a patient voice.

Eliza rested a hand on his arm. That was, perhaps, the only thing that truly steadied him. Shame over the strength of his reaction rushed in as his anger diminished, but it wasn't enough to silence his fury entirely. After everything Eliza had confessed to him, he was more determined to bring Ward to justice forever. He was determined to smash the man's balls open with a cricket

72

bat. But he needed Ivy to identify the bastard in order to give him the excuse.

"Where has she gone?" he asked in a quieter, though still demanding, voice, marching up the hall and back into the kitchen.

Rufus's staff must have heard his reaction. They were only pretending to do their work as they peeked at him, craning their necks to get a better look as he strode through the kitchen and into the downstairs hallway. He was somewhat satisfied when Moss, Rufus's butler, strode down the hall toward him with a look of concern that matched the situation.

"She was reported missing three hours ago," Moss said in a grave voice. "We have been searching high and low for her ever since."

"Why was I not informed?" Adolphus demanded.

Moss flushed and cleared his throat. "You were otherwise engaged, sir."

A completely incongruous feeling of sheepishness cut through Adolphus's rage. He'd been enjoying himself with Eliza and cleaning up in the aftermath while his key witness slipped out of everyone's grasp. Chances were, she'd seen Ward arrive and had bolted. He damned his own hide for losing focus and damned Ivy for losing her nerve and failing to trust that he and Rufus would protect her.

"Right," he said, taking charge of the situation. "We must find her. The sooner the better."

"Yes, sir." Moss nodded. "I have as many footmen as

can be spared searching as we speak. Supper needs to be served—"

"I don't care about supper," Adolphus snapped. "Miss Ivy is our first priority."

"The rest of my guests may disagree with you, mate," Rufus said uncomfortably.

"He's right," Eliza added.

Adolphus puffed out a breath, running a hand through his hair. He had to admit that he wasn't in London, with a devoted cadre of Runners at his beck and call. He was at a salacious house party, full of hungry guests who would want their soup on time.

"The more we make it seem as though everything is sailing on as smoothly as usual, the more likely Henry is to stay put and let his guard down," Eliza continued in a quiet voice.

Adolphus studied her. He hated hearing her use the bastard's given name. Hard as she was being on herself, it was obvious to him that Ward had abused her in the worst way possible. Not only did he want to see the devil slapped behind bars or transported to Australia, he wanted to wipe away the memories of his crime from Eliza's heart, to show her that not all men saw her as a whore because she had once been taken advantage of. Dammit, he wanted to marry her.

"Carry on with supper," he said at last, blowing out a breath and letting his shoulders drop. "If you can spare any staff at all to aid in the search, I would be grateful."

"I'll see what I can do, sir," Moss said. He bowed, then rushed off on his errand.

"I can question some of the female guests," Eliza said. "Miss Ivy might have felt safer going to them for help. Women tend to notice each other far more than men notice us. Someone may have made note of her running off to what she would consider a safe spot."

"And I'll head out to the stables to see if Tom Hastings has seen her," Rufus said.

Adolphus frowned at him in confusion.

"Tom helped her get settled that first day," Rufus explained with a shrug. "I've heard they continued to talk."

Adolphus wasn't sure if he welcomed that revelation or whether he wanted to roll his eyes over it. The last thing they needed was more romantic entanglements.

All the same, he nodded. "We need to move. The sooner we find Miss Ivy, the sooner she can identify Ward from the London incident and the sooner that worm can be brought to justice."

He glanced to Eliza. Her face had gone pink. She nodded to him as though she understood just how desperate he was to punish the man. If he could have taken the fear out of her eyes and her heart, he would have moved mountains to do so. She was his to care for and protect, whether she knew it yet or not.

They broke apart, each of them going their different ways. Adolphus hated leaving Eliza's side, but she was right about women noticing other women where men didn't, and it was far more likely a woman would share information with her if he, a man, were not present.

That left him to wander the house, looking into every room he could find, on his own. His years as a Runner had taught him that no room was ever truly empty and that even a peaceful house was brimming with activity in the corners where no one was looking. He found far more than anyone would have expected in his wandering.

"So the deal is done, then?" he heard Lord Marlowe ask as he drew near to a small parlor in the west wing.

"As done as could be," Mr. Pigge, the sour old merchant who had prattled on endlessly about the commercial empire he planned to establish in America, answered. "I don't care which of your daughters you give me, though. They're each as tasty as the next."

"That they are," Lord Marlowe chuckled. "Sometimes I despair that they are my own flesh and blood. It would be a treat to consider them as something else."

"I know men who do it," Mr. Pigge said in a voice that was far too casual. "And why not? What young miss is going to admit to relations with her father."

Lord Marlowe's answering hum of consideration turned Adolphus's blood cold. The only thing that stopped him from barging into the room and throttling the blackguard was his sigh as he continued with, "Let it be Lettuce, then. She's the eldest and prettiest. Alice is already more or less promised to Count Camoni, and my friend Cunningham has his sights set on Imogen. Lettuce will suit you well in America."

"I only need her to spread her legs and give me a son or two," Mr. Pigge said. "And I will thoroughly enjoy the process."

The two men chuckled. Adolphus sneered in disgust and pushed on. As much as he wanted to teach the two men a lesson in decency, legally, he couldn't interfere in any marriage brokering a Lord would do for his daughters.

The far reaches of the house were quieter than usual as party guests assembled for supper. It gave Adolphus all the latitude he needed to check private parlors, to look into bedrooms upstairs, and to rifle through Ward's things. The bastard had yet to unpack, but he hadn't brought much to begin with. The room Ward had been given was decorated in shades of pink and red, giving Adolphus the sense that it hadn't been intended for guest occupancy, but rather for the sort of mischief he and Eliza had gotten up to in the servants' hall. That left him wondering how many bedrooms had been set up throughout the house for exactly that kind of behavior.

His final check of the room before leaving brought him to an ornate cabinet in one corner. It was made of cherry wood and inlaid with hearts and flowers and other ornate nonsense. When he tried to open it, though, he discovered it was locked. The keyhole was surrounded by more hearts and frippery. It seemed ridiculous for such a piece to exist in the first place. He couldn't imagine what mysteries the cabinet contained.

Miss Ivy wasn't hiding in any of the guest bedrooms.

Adolphus decided that much after a relatively short search. He continued down to the east wing of the house, looking into more parlors and what looked like a billiard's room.

The billiard's room wasn't empty. The moment he stepped inside, a young couple by the window jumped apart. Adolphus recognized Lady Imogen Marlowe and Lord Thaddeus Herrington, Rufus's younger brother, in an instant. He'd had his hand on her waist and her hand had been tucked under the hem of his coat, but they reeled back from each other so fast that Adolphus had no doubt the two were engaged in some sort of mischief. Thaddeus's face burned as red as his hair, and Lady Imogen turned away in embarrassment.

"I beg your pardon," Adolphus said, bowing, then quickly leaving the room. He grinned to himself as he went. If Lord Marlowe thought he was going to be able to palm his youngest daughter off on an old goat like Lord Cunningham, he had better think again.

More than an hour later, without so much as a hint of Miss Ivy in the entire breadth of the house, Adolphus gave up. He waylaid the nearest servant he could find and asked them to have a light supper sent up to his room. He couldn't bear to sit down at a table with over fifty people, making small talk while his case spun wildly out of control. All he wanted to do was retire for the evening and concentrate on how he was going to convince Eliza to marry him. Her reticence baffled him. He might not have been a titled gentleman, but he had money enough. He could provide her with a comfortable life, a safe life. He would fill her nights with pleasure and her womb with babies. He would—

"I didn't think you would ever come back here," Eliza herself said, rising from one of the chairs by the fireplace in his bedroom as soon as he opened the door.

Adolphus rushed inside and shut the door, wary of anyone seeing her in his bedroom. Particularly since she appeared to be wearing nothing but the robe she'd taken from the wardrobe in the upstairs room.

"Eliza. What are you doing here?" he asked, crossing the room to her.

"Waiting for you," she answered, rising and meeting him by slipping her arms over his shoulders.

The only natural response was to close his arms around her waist and pull her close. The moment their bodies met, even though there were layers of clothes between them, desire coursed through him. His cock started to go rigid and his heart sped up. He attempted to force himself to stay focused.

"Did you locate Miss Ivy or any information pertaining to her?" he asked.

"No," she sighed. The subtle way her body sagged in his arms accelerated his process of arousal. "None of the female guests I spoke to have seen her. None of them even knew who she was."

Adolphus's disappointment was clouded by heat as she threaded her fingers through his hair. "Why are you not at supper with the other guests?" he asked, his voice rough.

She answered his question with a grin that made him want to tug loose her robe and ravish her. "I would rather be here with you," she said, lifting to her toes. Her lips were a breath away from his when she rocked back to her feet and said, "Caro wanted me to tell you that she's convinced Henry to stay the night at least. She says you will have to act fast to find Miss Ivy, because she cannot guarantee his continued presence in Shropshire."

If anything could have doused his increasing arousal, that was it. He let go of Eliza, pacing toward the fireplace and scrubbing his hands across his face. "I will not give up this case, not after coming so far. If I have to wrestle Ward into a trunk and transport him back to London on the back of a camel so that others can identify him, I will."

"Camels in England?" Eliza grinned, following him to the fireplace. "That is a sight I would like to see." She reached him, and her hands went straight to the buttons of his coat. "Now, let's make you a bit more comfortable."

"Eliza," he started, clearing his throat. That was as far as his thoughts extended, though. Her deft fingers making quick work of the buttons of his coat and waistcoat made it nearly impossible for him to think. He wanted to vow to her that he would bring Ward to justice, not just for the sake of the man he'd killed outside the pub, but for her and any other woman he'd importuned in the same way. He wanted to expound on all the ways that she was beautiful and worthy. What he ended up blurting was, "Marry me."

Her hands paused in their work and she glanced slowly up at him. "Why?" she asked, cunning in her eyes.

He blinked. "Because I can keep you safe. I can give you a comfortable home and children. You will never have to deal with the likes of Ward again."

She answered by glancing down in disappointment. "No. Not for those reasons."

After the intensity of the day he'd had, her answer felt like a cannon exploding in his mind. "What is wrong with my reasons?" he demanded. "They are perfectly reasonable reasons."

He rolled his eyes at himself inwardly. He was beginning to sound like the impertinent, dissatisfied boy he'd been when his father had insisted he was not cut out to become a Runner and should instead settle for a clerical job, like his brothers.

Eliza's answer was cut off before she could do more than open her mouth as a quiet knock sounded at the door. Adolphus let out an impatient breath and strode to answer it.

"Your supper, sir." An exhausted footman presented him with a tray containing a plate of meat, cheese, and bread, and a pot of tea.

Adolphus took it from him with a curt nod. The footman glanced to his undone buttons, past his shoulder to Eliza, then grinned. He nodded, then stepped away from the door as if he knew full well he was intruding.

Adolphus sighed as he shut the door with his foot, then carried the tray to the table in the corner. "You're welcome to any of this," he told Eliza over his shoulder.

She surprised him by flying back into his arms, nearly tackling him as she did. "The only thing I want to feast on is you," she said, pushing his coat from his shoulders.

"You're not hungry?" he asked, questioning which he himself wanted to eat more—the food or her pussy.

"I'm hungry for you," she said, peeling off his waistcoat.

A thousand thoughts zipped through Adolphus's mind at once. He should behave honorably toward her. He wanted to fuck her in every way possible. Venting his lust on her might only exacerbate her poor opinion of herself. He could change that opinion by showing her how desirable she truly was. They should eat supper before the tea grew cold.

He latched on to his second-to-last thought, stepping away from the table and pulling her into his arms. One tug was all it took to open the front of her robe. As he expected, she was naked underneath. He spread his hand across her bare back, lowering it to cup her backside, and slanted his mouth over hers.

The sounds of pleasure she made as he kissed her, pouring his whole heart and soul into the mating of their mouths, had his cock as hard as marble in an instant. Was he a devil for delighting in how open and sensual she was? Did it make him as horrid as the men who had taken advantage of her sensuality in the past?

No. He couldn't believe he was that evil. The key was not to steal pleasure from her but to aid her in enjoying her own hot-blooded nature. He squeezed her backside, grinding his erection against her so that she could see what she did to him. It was all her handiwork, and he would show her just how much he appreciated it.

"Fuck me," she sighed against his cheek as she tugged his shirt from his breeches. "I want to feel you hard and rough inside of me."

"No," he said, brushing his hands up her sides, over her breasts, and to her shoulders to push her robe off. When she flinched back in surprise, staring at him with wide, confused eyes, he said, "I am going to make love to you, slowly and gently. I'm going to make you feel things no other man has made you feel."

She flushed. Curiosity and arousal were bright in her eyes, and with them a kind of tenderness that broke Adolphus's heart. It wasn't just her body that other men had abused shamelessly, it was her sweet nature and her gentleness.

He pulled her against him once more, kissing her with a slower, smoldering passion. His blood pounded and his cock demanded satisfaction, but he let his heart rule the rest of him. He teased his hands across her skin, almost tickling her, instead of clamping or grasping. He slipped his tongue alongside hers, drawing moans from deep within her. Then he trailed soft kisses across her neck and shoulder until he had her back arched so that he could flicker his tongue across her nipple before drawing it into his mouth to tease with his teeth.

"Oh, oh," she panted, breathless.

In spite of his plans, he wasn't certain how long he would be able to last. Speed was of the essence. He lifted her, carrying her to the bed and laying her as gently as he could across the coverlet. She was a picture of carnal beauty and bliss as she wriggled into the center of the bed while he shed the rest of his clothes. She was clearly posing for him in the most erotic way possible, parting her legs to show him her glistening cunny. But at the same time, there was a sort of shyness in her movements, and she closed her legs as easily as she'd opened them. It was as though she had attempted her usual, siren's routine, only to realize she was in an entirely new situation where boldness wasn't required. Her hesitation and her paradoxical innocence drove him wild.

She sat up when he tossed the last of his clothes aside and approached the bed. "I adore your cock," she said, her eyes hungry as she stared at his straining erection. "I want to play with it, swallow it."

She reached for him as he joined her on the bed, but he pushed her hands away. "Some other time," he said, nudging her to her back once more. "I will let you torture me with your hands and mouth in any way you wish to, as long as it is truly what you wish to do and not merely something you think you should do, but not now. Not tonight."

"But—"

He silenced her with a kiss, spreading his body carefully over hers and drinking the sound of protest away from her lips. She was left humming with pleasure. She opened her hips to him, drawing her legs up to his sides in a clear invitation.

He accepted her invitation, but not in the way he was certain she meant it. He broke away from her mouth, slowly kissing his way down her body in a way designed to give her as much pleasure as possible. He lingered on her magnificent breasts, licking, teasing, and suckling her nipples into tautness. If she could play with his cock for hours, he was certain he could do the same with her breasts, but they were only a leisurely stop on his journey across her body, not his destination.

She mewled and sighed as he made his way across her belly, arching into his kisses. The way she stretched her arms over her head and wriggled with a special kind of desperation told him he was accomplishing exactly what he'd set out to do. By the time he reached her hips and stroked her thighs, spreading them as far as he could, she seemed to be near weeping with pleasure. Her slit was slick with wetness, pink and ready. He warned himself to proceed carefully so as not to make her come too quickly.

She tasted like life itself as he flickered his tongue across her opening, earning a gasp of delight from her. She continued to pant and move so restlessly that he was forced to grip her thighs far tighter than he had a mind to simply to keep her from arching off the bed. He buried his face in her mound, stroking her with his tongue and teasing her clitoris until he sensed she was about to break. Then he backed away, watching her aroused flesh until the imminent danger had passed. Then he delved into her once more, bringing her as close to the brink as he dared, only to pull away again and wait.

"Dear God, you're driving me mad," she groaned after his third ministration. "Please, please let me come."

"Not yet," he said, blowing gently on her exposed sex. "It will be so much better this way."

She groaned with a sensual combination of misery and lust as he moved in to tease her for a fourth time. Her every movement, every sound she made and twitch of her body brought him closer and closer to his own limit. He ached to find his home within her and to feel the rush of pleasure that came with spilling his seed inside of her. And he would spend inside of her, selfish as it was. He wanted to stay with her always, in big ways and in small.

He knew it was time to end things with astounding pleasure when he lifted his head to watch her body writhing in pleasure, her face contorted with need. Her breasts were flushed, her nipples pointing straight up. It was a sight he couldn't resist. When he went down on her next, he did so without teasing or mischief, but with the expressed purpose of making her come spectacularly, which she did within seconds. She let out a heartfelt cry of release as her body throbbed into orgasm.

He wasted no time. With a powerful movement, he pulled himself up the length of her body and lodged himself deep within her with a cry. Her inner muscles squeezed him in the most delicious way possible. He wanted to hold himself still within her to enjoy every moment, but he couldn't help but move. He needed to mate with her, needed to give himself to her in every way. He needed to be hers.

Orgasm crashed through him with the full force of the emotions that gripped his heart far faster than he would have liked. The glorious exchange of tension and power for release and surrender was almost too much for him. He called out wordlessly as what felt like a part of himself left him for her. It was beyond joy, beyond satisfaction. It was heaven.

Release left him sated and heavy. He sagged to her side, desperate to catch his breath. He was beyond words, but she seemed to be as well. All he could do was shift her into his arms as he rolled to his back and closed his eyes. He wanted to tell her how much she meant to him, how much he cared about her, but all he could manage was to close his eyes and cling to her as sleep overtook him.

CHAPTER 7

*E*liza couldn't explain why she felt so shy the next morning. She woke with the sun—or what had been passing for sun in the cold and rainy summer—nestled against Adolphus's side, feeling safer than she ever had. She'd slept far longer than she should have, which was likely a product of that safe feeling. Adolphus was already awake, but didn't seem in any hurry to rouse her or get up.

Once she was roused, he made no attempt to roll her to her back to make love to her again or order her to leave his bed, or even to chastise her for being such a wanton the night before. He merely shifted so that he could kiss her lips lightly, told her good morning, then asked, "Will you marry me now?"

Somehow, in her hazy, morning state, she had enough presence of mind to ask, "Why do you want to marry me?"

A stern look came over Adolphus's face, as though his patience for her games were wearing thin. But Eliza was fairly impressed with his answer of, "Because we belong together."

She smiled. She kissed him in return. Then she rolled away from him, climbing out of the bed and bending to retrieve her clothes. It still wasn't the answer she wanted, but it was good enough for her not to turn him down outright.

"Eliza?" he asked, getting out of bed and striding around to face her.

The sight of him naked, even if he wasn't fully aroused, was enough to steal Eliza's breath. He was the handsomest man she'd ever seen in every way. She would marry him, of course, if only because she wanted to be able to brag to all of the ladies of the *ton* who had turned up their noses at her and made her a pariah that she had ended up with a kinder, cleverer, handsomer husband than any of them. Even if it meant she would be Lady Eliza no more and only Mrs. Gibbon. There was nothing wrong with Mrs. Gibbon, particularly since Lady Eliza had never truly fit into her surroundings.

"We should resume the search for Miss Ivy as quickly as possible," she said instead of answering what he clearly wanted to know about her answer to his proposal.

For a moment, he looked as though he would protest. But as Eliza suspected was always the case with him, duty won out over his heart. "You are right," he said, crossing to his washstand. "The sooner we can conclude this mess with Ward, the sooner we will be able to have the reckoning that is becoming increasingly necessary."

Why his words sent a delighted chill down her back, Eliza didn't know. Perhaps it was the formality of the way he spoke. Perhaps it was the delicious foreshadowing in his tone. Or perhaps it was the way that he glanced sternly at her over his shoulder as he set about his morning ablutions—as if a reckoning would involve her submitting to him in ways that left her desperate with pleasure, as she had been the night before. Whatever the case, she looked forward to it.

She slipped back to her room, managing not to be seen, so that she could wash and dress in a fresh gown herself. Part of her wanted to stay with Adolphus, but she knew too well that if she started out scrubbing a wet sponge over her heated body with him in the same room, they would end up back in bed. She might have used the search for Miss Ivy as an excuse not to answer him about marriage, but the young barmaid truly did need to be found. Adolphus was right, the sooner they concluded matters with Henry and had the bastard taken back to London to stand trial, the quicker everything could move on.

Henry wasn't in the breakfast room when Eliza made her way down to find sustenance for the day ahead. In spite of the veritable feast laid out on the sideboard, only a handful of guests were there to eat.

"It's because most everyone has continued with the hunt," Ophelia whispered to her as Eliza took a place at the table. Mr. Saif Khan sat on her other side, seemingly more interested in studying Ophelia's curves than buttering the bun in his hands. "No one has found the prize yet," Ophelia went on. "I know of at least half a dozen couples who have already resumed their search."

"We should follow their example soon," Mr. Khan said, his smile eager, as though there were other things he would like to get on with where Ophelia was concerned.

Eliza peeked farther down the table, where Adolphus was seated, talking to Lord Herrington with a frown. He'd already been seated at the table when Eliza entered the room, but even though they'd arrived separately, she had a feeling that their night's activity was a secret to no one. He must have felt her looking, because he glanced up at her. Miraculously, as soon as their eyes met, a gentle smile curved his lips.

Eliza's heart ricocheted against her ribs as she went back to eating her breakfast. She couldn't remove the smile from her face, though. It was still there, showing all the world just what she thought of Adolphus, as they finished their meal and met up in the hallway just outside of the breakfast room.

"Where should we begin our search?" she whispered. If not for the handful of other guests wandering around them, she would have thrown herself into his arms and asked the question with an entirely different meaning.

"We should question the servants once again," Adolphus said, taking her hand and leading her down the hall toward the servants' stairs. "Something may have transpired in the night that will shed light on Miss Ivy's whereabouts."

Eliza was certain he was right, but before they could travel more than halfway down the hall, Caro stepped out of one of the multitude of parlors, her eyes wide and her color high, to stop them.

"What perfect luck," she said, taking hold of Eliza's arm and leading her away from Adolphus and into the parlor. Adolphus followed with a frown. "I was hoping to find the two of you continuing the hunt," Caro went on. "You are just what Lady Rothsay and Mr. Ward need to aid their search."

The hair on the back of Eliza's neck stood up as she came face to face with Henry in the small parlor. He looked more than a bit put out, and the air of anxiety hovering around him intensified when Adolphus came to a stop just behind Eliza. He seemed so startled that Eliza was certain he would bolt.

Caro had other plans, though. "You see, Mr. Ward?" she asked as though she and Henry had been having a much longer conversation. "Mr. Gibbon and Lady Eliza are more than willing to aid you and Lady Rothsay in your hunt."

"I beg your pardon?" Eliza asked. If Caro wanted to throw her into some sort of game with Henry, she needed to be certain she knew what it was.

As genteel and smooth as Caro's expression was, the spark of ingenuity—not to mention panic—was bright in her eyes. "I am afraid Lady Rothsay's partner for the hunt has dropped out after a small prank by the Trickster left him with a twisted ankle yesterday."

"Lord Campbell was forced to leap from the top of a wardrobe, where we were trapped, to retrieve the ladder that enabled me to climb down," Lady Rothsay said with a flat, sideways look at Caro.

"Oh, dear." Eliza didn't know whether to laugh or be shocked.

"But fortunately, Mr. Ward arrived yesterday to even the teams once more," Caro went on.

"As I have tried to explain, my lady," Henry said, his jaw tight, "I have no wish to partake of these festivities. I really should be on my way back to London." He glanced askance to Adolphus.

"And as I have told you, my dear Mr. Ward, your horse is in no condition to make the journey as of yet, and the problems we've been having with highwaymen are too acute for you to leave so soon," Caro said, her cheeks growing pinker by the moment. "And Lady Rothsay is in need of a partner."

"They do say the prize at the end of this hunt is a king's ransom," Lady Rothsay said, a hint of avarice in her eyes.

Surprisingly, Henry seemed to respond to that. "A king's ransom, you say?"

"I am not at liberty to divulge any secrets," Caro answered, doing a terrible job of hiding just how valuable the prize was with her look. Or perhaps she was doing a splendid job of acting as though the prize was at the fore-front of her thoughts.

"Well," Henry began, rubbing his chin.

"It's settled, then." Caro took Henry's arm and led him to Lady Rothsay. "The hunt continues. I took the liberty of retrieving the clue you discovered yesterday, Mr. Gibbon, which would have led you on to the same path as Lady Rothsay and Lord Campbell were about to find themselves on."

Eliza doubted that was true, but she didn't protest as Caro withdrew the waxy slip of paper that was their clue from the servants' room and handed it to Adolphus. Before Adolphus could do more than frown, Caro hooked her arm through Eliza's and tugged her to the side.

"I just need to have a word about a personal matter with Lady Eliza," Caro explained in a whisper. "By all means, continue with the clue among yourselves."

"What is the meaning of this?" Eliza hissed when they reached the corner of the room. "I have no wish to spend so much as a moment in Henry Ward's company."

"You must keep him interested in the hunt," Caro whispered back. "Rufus caught him trying to leave once again this morning. Keep him busy. Convince him that Mr. Gibbon is here for diversion and amusement only. We have every able-bodied person we can spare searching for Miss Ivy."

"And if you fail to find her?" Eliza asked.

Caro pressed her lips together. "We will find her. Keep Mr. Ward busy until we do."

With a quick squeeze of her hands, Caro broke away from Eliza and started out of the room.

"Enjoy your hunt," she said with a charming smile, then bolted.

Eliza frowned, a sick feeling in the pit of her stomach that made her wish she hadn't eaten so much of her breakfast. She glanced to Adolphus, who stared back at her questioningly.

"The clue, the clue," Lady Rothsay said with an irritated sigh. "What does the clue say."

Eliza walked back to join the others as Adolphus cleared his throat and read, "I can be found where little feet patter. Play the game and you will spot me."

"This is foolish," Henry grumbled.

"Whatever could it mean?" Lady Rothsay said, taking the clue from Adolphus and frowning at it.

"The clue is in a nursery of some sort," Adolphus said, his frown as sour as the tone of his voice.

"Yes, of course." Lady Rothsay smiled. "Where is the nursery?"

"I have no wish to know," Henry said, starting away from them. "I don't care what Lady Herrington says, I'm not staying here."

"Oh, but you must," Eliza blurted before she could think better of it. She glanced to Adolphus, then hurried after Henry, catching his arm. "The party would not truly be a party without you."

Henry stopped, then slowly turned to study her. He glanced down at her hand on his arm, then raked his gaze up over her chest, to meet her eyes with a wolfish hunger. "So you've changed your mind, have you?"

Eliza could practically feel Adolphus's fury behind her. "Yes," she said with a smile that she hoped appeared genuine. "We must find the prize, after all. And now we have an advantage—four people searching together instead of just two."

"Yes, well, there is the prize." Henry rubbed his chin, glancing at her chest.

"It should not take long to find the nursery," Adolphus grumbled, marching up behind Eliza. He took her arm, pulling her away from Henry and practically shoving her out to the hall.

Eliza had never been so happy to be manhandled. "Is he following?" she whispered as they made their way to the grand staircase in the front hall.

Adolphus checked over his shoulder then answered, "Yes."

By the time they made their way up to the second floor and found the nursery, tucked away at the far end of the east wing, Henry had relaxed into the game somewhat. Eliza was far from relaxed, though she did her best to pretend otherwise.

"Which game do you suppose we must play to find the next clue?" she asked as the four of them stood near the door to the nursery.

Though Caro and Rufus had no children as of yet and Rufus's siblings were all too old for a nursery, the room was arranged as though for immediate occupation. A child's size table sat in the middle of the room with tiny chairs around it. Painted wooden blocks were scattered across the tabletop, waiting to be built with. A magnificent doll's house sat in one corner of the room, its furnishings beautiful and elaborate, a family of dolls sitting in the tiny parlor. A slate and tray of chalk stood against one wall, half the alphabet already written out. Various other toys—from balls to hoops to dolls—were scattered around the room.

"We may have to play all of them," Eliza said, wondering what Caro had had in mind for her guests before the urgency of Henry had turned things sour.

"Nonsense," Henry said. "I'm not going to waste my time playing children's games."

"You aren't man enough?" Adolphus asked.

Henry's transformation was astounding. Eliza couldn't have coaxed him into action in any better way. The air of nervousness about him vanished, replaced by furious challenge. He glared at Adolphus as though they'd decided on pistols at dawn.

"What do you plan to do, sir?" he asked. "Play with dolls?"

"If it will lead me to the prize before anyone else, yes," Adolphus answered, then marched straight across the room to the dollhouse.

Eliza giggled before she could stop herself and followed him. The sight of large, strong Adolphus, Bow Street Runner, sitting on the floor in front of a magnificently feminine dollhouse and snatching up the father doll was enough to warm her heart for years to come.

Not to be outdone, Henry stomped his way to the table, pulling out one of the tiny chairs, and sitting in it. He looked like a giant trying to fit in among humans as he reached for some of the blocks on the table and began turning them over. Lady Rothsay rushed to his aid, sitting just as humorously as he was.

"The clue is likely hidden inside of one of these toys," Eliza whispered as she took up one of the dolls and checked under her skirts.

"Yes," Adolphus agreed. "But is this enough of a diversion to keep Ward occupied?"

They both looked over his shoulders to where Henry and Lady Rothsay were turning over every block on the table, and even tapping them to be certain none were boxes in disguise.

"It seems to be working well so far," Eliza said.

Adolphus hummed noncommittally as he took a sofa out of the dollhouse parlor and turned it over, checking for clues. He followed that by lifting the rug, then checking behind the tiny bookshelf.

Eliza took a different approach. "Dear me, wherever could I have left my clue?" she said in a childlike voice, miming a search of the dining room with the mother doll. "It must be here somewhere."

Adolphus sent her a flat look as she pranced the doll through the dining room, as if the doll were searching. "We don't have time for silliness," he said.

"But is the whole thing not silliness?" she said, still miming with the doll instead of speaking to him directly.

Adolphus sighed, taking the father doll and standing him in front of Eliza's doll in the dining room. "Life is not silly," he said through the doll, though without changing his voice. "It is hard work and effort."

"But there must be time for fun as well," Eliza had her doll say.

"If you want fun," Adolphus began, moving his doll out of the dining room and into the dollhouse bedroom.

Eliza laughed, putting her doll in the bedroom as well. "Yes, please, Mr. Gibbon," she said, miming her doll rushing across the room and throwing herself at Adolphus's doll.

She would have carried on, in spite of the fact that Henry and Lady Rothsay had moved on to searching the pile of dolls and soft toys in the far corner of the room, except for the harried-looking hall boy that dashed into the room and straight over to Adolphus.

"If you please, sir," the boy said, thrusting a hand with a folded piece of paper in it at Adolphus.

Adolphus abandoned his doll and turned to take the note from the boy. If the boy saw anything odd in a large man sitting on the floor of a nursery playing with a dollhouse, he didn't say. He turned and dashed out of the room immediately.

Adolphus glanced to Eliza before opening the note. Eliza shifted so that she could read it as he did.

"*Beggn yer pardn, mister Gibbn, sir. I saw mister*

Ward arrive an got scred if he cees me heel kilt me like he dun Bob. I gone int hydn, but ye cn find mee wit the pryz at the end o the hunt."

"What the devil," Adolphus grumbled.

"Miss Ivy is hiding with the prize at the end of the hunt?" Eliza asked in a low voice.

"You," Henry called from across the room, leaving the dolls and marching toward them. "Are you cheating? What did that boy bring you?"

"Business," Adolphus said, rushing to stand.

"I think you're cheating," Henry insisted as Eliza scrambled to her feet as well. "Let me see the clue. Let me see it."

Eliza caught her breath, certain there would be a fight and that Henry would run.

The only thing that stopped the inevitable was Lady Rothsay's sudden shriek. Eliza was convinced the woman had hurt herself until she straightened, brandishing a slip of paper. "I found it," she squealed. "I found the next clue."

Henry glared at Adolphus, then twisted to face Lady Rothsay, as if torn.

Lady Rothsay opened the folded paper and read in a rushed, breathless voice, "I am the pride of Iberia, friend of Lope de Vega and Miguel de Cervantes. Find me and you will find glory."

"Is that it?" Eliza asked. "Is that the final clue?"

"She is with the prize," Adolphus said, barely audible.

Henry must have heard part of his statement but perhaps not all of it. He narrowed his eyes. "You do want to win the prize, don't you?"

A flush painted Adolphus's cheeks. "Any man would be a fool not to want great wealth," he said.

Henry's entire demeanor changed. Suddenly, it seemed as though he thought of Adolphus entirely as a rival—for the prize and perhaps for Eliza—not a Runner who might bring him to justice. And as with every man Eliza had ever known, now that he saw Adolphus differently, the flash of competition was hot in his eyes.

"You won't win," he said.

"I will." Adolphus stepped toe to toe with him. "Because I know what the clue is referring to." He broke into a sly grin.

"The Spanish parlor," Lady Rothsay blurted, ruining Adolphus's upper hand. "The next clue is in the Spanish parlor."

Eliza would have rolled her eyes at the woman's outburst, but there was no time. Instantly, they all dashed into motion, running for the door.

CHAPTER 8

$\mathcal{I}$t was a mad scramble, worthy of the children who had once occupied the nursery. In spite of the dread of having Henry as part of her group, in spite of the ache of old memories he'd brought up, and in spite of her sizzling feelings toward Adolphus, Eliza found herself giggling like mad along with Lady Rothsay as the two of them raced downstairs and through the halls toward the Spanish parlor.

"This is well beneath my dignity," Lady Rothsay laughed as the two of them skidded around the final corner, Adolphus and Henry jogging to keep up. "A widow of my age...."

"We are only young once, but we can be immature forever," Eliza told her as they skidded to a halt in front of the door to the Spanish parlor.

Lady Rothsay laughed aloud, but quickly swallowed

the sound at the sight of the forbidding butler who stood solidly in front of the Spanish parlor's doors.

"Let us through," Adolphus said, eyeing the butler with particular vehemence.

"Begging your pardon, sir," the butler said, "but I have been instructed to inform you that this entrance to the Spanish parlor is unavailable at the moment, and that you may enter through the adjacent parlor."

Eliza remembered all about the adjacent parlor. It was the space where Felicity had lured Lord Cunningham into humiliating himself in front of a crowd of party guests waiting for an evening's entertainment. She broke away from the door and the others and hurried several yards along the hall to the smaller parlor's door.

Once again, however, she and the others were met with a surprise.

"Actors only?" Lady Rothsay read the sign that hung on the door. "Whatever does that mean?"

"No good, I'm certain," Adolphus said, resting a hand on the small of Eliza's back. It was a simple gesture, but it spoke volumes about the way Adolphus's patience was running out and how much he cared for Eliza's well-being in the mad hunt.

"Are you a coward, Gibbon?" Henry asked. For the first time since he'd arrived at the house party, his expression was one of fun and excitement without any of the anxiety or suspicion he'd developed since discovering Adolphus.

"Hardly," Adolphus growled, then turned the handle and pushed the door open.

The moment the four of them stepped into the small parlor, pandemonium reigned.

"You're late, you're late," Rufus announced, grabbing each one in turn and shoving them deeper into the room, toward his brother Thaddeus and Lady Imogen Marlowe —who were beside themselves with giggles as they pulled what appeared to be costumes out of a large trunk. "The curtains will part in a matter of moments. You will receive your final clue once the play is done."

"Once the play is done?" Henry protested, attempting to bat away Rufus's shoves as they were herded toward the costume trunk.

"Yes, yes," Rufus went on, playing the part of the director to perfection. "Here are your scripts. All you need to do is read the lines that have been highlighted for you." He shoved thin scripts into each of their hands even as Thaddeus began tossing costumes in their direction.

"At least the play is short," Adolphus grumbled, then balked at the script he'd been handed. "Hang on. Dulcinea?"

"Don Quixote," Lady Rothsay exclaimed, bursting into laughter once more.

"Is that the play we are meant to perform?" Eliza glanced at the front page of her script.

"No, that is the role I have been given," Lady Rothsay went on.

"Oh." Rufus seemed a bit disappointed. "I may have given you the wrong script."

He made a move toward Eliza, but before he could do more, Lady Rothsay clutched her script to her chest. "Oh no. I have always wanted to play the lead in a theatrical production. I shall be the best Don Quixote any stage has ever seen."

Eliza's grin grew as she saw the name "Sancho" on her script. "And I shall be your faithful servant," she said, skipping to Lady Rothsay's side.

"I will not play a female role," Adolphus protested.

But it was already too late. Thaddeus came at him with what appeared to be a bundle of rose-colored fabric which he tossed over Adolphus's head. The fabric turned out to be a dress, and before Adolphus could do more than squirm and flail in an attempt to prevent himself from being dressed in the costume, it was too late.

"Fine," he sighed, as irritated as Eliza had ever seen him. "I will indulge in this farce if it results in us being given the final clue."

Imogen gestured for Eliza and Lady Rothsay to join her at the costume trunk, where they were handed trousers and doublets, as Henry roared with laughter. Unlike Lady Rothsay's laughter, his was bitterly unkind as he pointed at Adolphus.

"You look like a first-rate pouf," he snorted.

Adolphus looked as though he wanted to murder the man—which Eliza knew full well he already wanted to do for other reasons—until Thaddeus sheathed him in a costume as well.

"Hang on," Henry shouted as it became clear he, too, had been shoved into a dress. He checked the script in his hand. "Nurse?" he snapped. "Who the devil is the nurse?"

"You are," Rufus told him, forcing Henry's arms into his dress's sleeves then spinning him to tie it in the back. Once that was done, he clapped loudly and declared, "Places everyone."

Eliza finished putting on her breeches, then dashed over to Adolphus's side while doing up her doublet. "The play cannot be more than five pages," she whispered to him, having an impossible time not bursting into giggles. "All we have to do is say the lines, rush through, and then receive our clue."

"This is ridiculous," Adolphus said. "Worse than being forced to play with dolls."

Eliza arched a brow. "No one forced you to play with the dolls."

Adolphus answered with a wordless, noncommittal grumble.

"Let's get this over with," Henry sighed, letting Rufus lead him to a spot that was marked out with chalk on one side of the room, beside the heavy curtains.

Rufus positioned the others as well, all with a sense of haste and mischief. "Now," he said when they were all exactly where he wanted them. "I will give you the final clue if and only if you perform the play 'til its end. Is that understood?"

"Yes," Eliza and Lady Rothsay answered enthusiastically. Adolphus and Henry added grumbles that might have been assent.

"Very well then." Rufus stepped to the side, grabbed hold of the curtain's thick cords, and pulled. "You may begin."

Eliza checked her script to see who had the first line, but was instantly thrown by the swell of applause that followed in the wake of the curtain being opened.

Lady Rothsay exclaimed, "Good Lord."

Adolphus and Henry both let out oaths that were far stronger.

For there, spread out in front of them in the Spanish parlor proper, seated in at least a dozen rows, were the majority of the rest of the house party guests. They all wore smiles of expectation and seemed eager to see a show. Many of them were drinking tea and eating biscuits as they waited for things to begin, as if the play were more of a circus entertainment than a proper theatrical performance.

Of course, from the moment the curtain opened, very little happened other than the four of them standing there in their ridiculous costumes, gaping at the audience.

"Give us a show," someone shouted from the back of the room.

"Yes, we've been waiting here for an hour," a lady seconded him.

Most surprisingly of all, Lady Oliphant, the Duchess of Cavendish, who Eliza was surprised to see had returned to the house party, sat in the front row. She called out, "We've had three groups fail to perform for us already. Which, as I understand it, means they have dropped out of the competition for Lady Herrington's prize as well."

Eliza lit up at the comment and turned toward Adolphus. He was too far away from her for any sort of private exchange, but the time had passed for secrecy.

"That means we're close to winning," she said, stressing everything she wasn't saying aloud. "If we can just get through the play, we can *win the prize*." She stared hard at him, attempting to communicate *find Miss Ivy* instead.

Adolphus glared into the wings, where Rufus looked ready to burst. Rufus signaled for him to go on.

"Bloody hell," Adolphus grumbled, shocking a pair of younger ladies in the front row. He sighed heavily, then held up his script. "Señor Don Quixote, what brings you to my humble inn?" he read with absolutely no feeling whatsoever.

"It is not an inn, oh fairest of the fair," Lady Rothsay spoke her lines with vigor. "It is the fairest castle in the land, and you are the most beautiful maiden I have ever seen."

The audience laughed loud enough to shake the

chandeliers as Adolphus glared at his script, at Lady Rothsay, and at them. Eliza was convinced that the only thing that kept him going was Henry's sneer of amusement. Adolphus simply would not be cowed by the man.

"Sancho, is this not the most glorious maiden you have ever seen?" Lady Rothsay asked, getting even more into character.

Eliza was forced to pay attention to the script. "Oh, sir, she is just a humble servant of the inn." She crossed the stage, taking up a spot by Lady Rothsay's side.

"You cur," Lady Rothsay exclaimed.

The script called for Don Quixote to strike Sancho, so she raised her hand. With a wink to Eliza, she brought it down with exaggerated boldness. Eliza anticipated the blow and pretended to fall to the ground while Lady Rothsay's hand was still a good six inches from touching her. The audience burst into laughter. For extra measure, Eliza pretended to roll and thrash about on the floor in pain. The fun of being part of such a ridiculous play was a lark, and she was as inclined as Lady Rothsay was to enjoy it.

"What have you done, sir?" Henry asked in an improvised feminine voice that had their audience in stitches. He crossed the stage to kneel by Eliza's side. "Here. Let me tend to your wounds as I have tended to many a fine gentleman before you."

The humor of the moment vanished suddenly, even though the audience continued to laugh. Henry reached for her, closing his hands around her arms and maneuvering her into a position that was as suggestive as it was subservient. Memories of the past reached up to squeeze the air out of Eliza's lungs. It was all she could do to stop herself from weeping outright.

But Henry, most likely spurred on by the ribald laughter, milked the moment for all it was worth. He made it as clear as day what he was thinking when it came to his position relative to Eliza's. He even went so far as to push her flat to her back and to loom down over her.

All at once, he was wrenched away and the audience gasped. Adolphus had him by the back of his shirt and looked as though he would pummel the man into dust.

"How dare you lay a hand on her?" he demanded, turning Henry to face him and shaking him for all he was worth.

A murmur of excitement passed through the audience, and someone dropped their teacup, shattering it.

"You have treated Lady Eliza abominably," Adolphus raged on as Eliza scrambled to her feet, with Lady Rothsay's help. The two of them rushed to the side of the stage, out of the way of the men. "Don't think I don't know about your past with her."

"What did she tell you?" Henry demanded with something that might have been a laugh or a strangled cry of fear. "Did she tell you that she's a little whore who couldn't get enough of it?"

That was all it took. Adolphus threw a devastating punch that hit Henry square in the jaw, nearly spinning him in a circle. "I will not hear you speak ill of the woman I love," Adolphus roared. "You forced yourself on her, you miserable, pestilential cock." He threw a second punch that landed on Henry's ear.

Eliza was so stunned by Adolphus's words and his actions that she could only let her mouth drop open. Henry wasn't as stunned as she was, or as Adolphus might have thought he was. He recovered with a roar and charged at Adolphus, throwing punches of his own.

Within seconds, the two men were brawling as though they were behind a seedy pub in the dead of night. Two men dressed in silk and frills. The sickening crunch of punches being landed was matched only by the shouts of alarm—or encouragement—from the audience as ladies and gentlemen rose from their seats to either get away from the violence on the stage or to get a better look at the wild sight. Eliza flinched with every sound and every blow, especially when a bloom of red sprouted from Henry's nose and started to run down his face. At the same time, she was filled with immense satisfaction to see Adolphus taking the upper hand so easily.

At last, most likely sensing he was outmatched, Henry stumbled backward, holding up his hands. "I yield, I yield," he panted, then doubled over. "You can have the bitch."

Adolphus rushed toward him, a look of murder in his eyes. The only thing that stopped Henry from meeting his end was Rufus stepping between them.

"I must admit," he said in an overly loud voice, staring

hard at Adolphus, "an entertainment like this is even better than the play I wrote. I'll give you your clue so that you can move ahead and find the prize at last." He spoke deliberately and stared steadily at Adolphus as he did.

Eliza held her breath, wondering if Adolphus would choose direct revenge against Henry or if he would remember the mission they were on and follow Rufus's clue to locate Miss Ivy. Truly, she wondered why Rufus was not simply coming out and telling them where Miss Ivy was or bringing her forward. Then again, Henry had attempted to flee three times already, so perhaps continuing with the game was the only way to lead him where he needed to go.

"Give me the clue," Adolphus hissed at last, backing away from Rufus but keeping his fierce glare on Henry.

Rufus nodded, reaching into the pocket of his waistcoat.

"Hang on." Henry came forward, dabbing at his bleeding nose with the sleeve of his costume gown. "How is it fair to hand the clue over to him when he is the one who attacked me?"

"I believe, sir, that we both know you deserved it," Rufus said in a deadly voice, handing a folded slip of paper to Adolphus.

"What do you know about it?" Henry demanded, attempting to pull himself to his full height, but looking all the worse for it in his ripped, bloody dress, his nose and cheek swelling.

"I know more than you think I do," Rufus answered.

Henry laughed uneasily. "Did she tell you?" He pointed to Eliza. "I could tell you things about her that would make your hair turn white, friend. I could—"

Whatever Henry could do, they would never know. Adolphus crumpled the slip of paper in his bruised hand as he marched toward the door they'd entered the small parlor through.

"Wait," Eliza called, rushing after him. She gave Henry a look of absolute disgust as she passed him.

"You're not going on without me," Lady Rothsay said, leaping after her.

Henry followed after them, grumbling under his breath, "This isn't over yet."

CHAPTER 9

*F*inally. Finally, he was doing what came naturally to him. Finally, the blood was pumping through his veins and his muscles worked as he tore through the house, out the front door—which was manned by a footman who seemed to know Adolphus and the others would come tearing through at some point and held it wide open—and across the gravel drive toward the stables in back of the grand house. Finally, he was being the Runner that he was meant to be. The fact that he was doing his job while wearing an ill-fitting silk gown was beside the point.

Ward sprinted up behind him, clearly not as fit as Adolphus was but doing a fair job of holding his own. The man's face was a bloody mask from where Adolphus had broken his nose. Rather than feeling the slightest bit of guilt over causing such damage, Adolphus gloated over it. Ward deserved to have the structure of his face permanently altered in more ways than his broken nose would produce. The damage was worth every sore knuckle on his hand.

"Adolphus, wait," Eliza called from several yards behind him. "You're going too fast."

The guilt that Adolphus hadn't bothered to feel rose up in him. He was loath to leave Eliza behind—although she was doing an admirable job of keeping up with him in the costume breeches she wore. Far better than Lady Rothsay, who was puffing along at a good fifty yards' distance. But stopping to allow Eliza to catch up would mean allowing Ward to get ahead. And if Miss Ivy saw Ward coming on his own, she would likely bolt again.

He did the only thing he could do. He waited until Ward had caught up to his side, then rammed the bastard with his shoulder, sending him flying. Ward bellowed in wordless protest as he hit the ground. Adolphus took advantage of the moment to stop and turn back to Eliza.

"Hurry," he called. "We must get there first."

"Over my dead body," Ward growled.

Adolphus had miscalculated how injured and how pathetic Ward was. The bastard struggled to his knees and threw himself at Adolphus, catching him around his calves in a bear hug. It was impossible to stay upright under Ward's weight and momentum, and Adolphus tumbled to the ground. The moment of shock that followed provided just enough time for Ward to throw a punch that smashed across Adolphus's face.

"Ruin my nose, will you?" Ward barked, pulling back for another punch.

Adolphus was quicker and rolled out of the way, sending Ward off balance when his punch missed its target. He managed to twist back fast enough to pin Ward before he could sort himself out.

"You've ruined far more than a nose," Adolphus growled, pressing down on Ward's chest and hoping he couldn't breathe. "You ruined a beautiful, innocent girl." When Ward looked as though he would protest, Adolphus went on with, "Bastards like you know full well your attentions are not welcome, but you force them anyhow and blame the woman for being unable to defend herself."

"Adolphus!"

Eliza's shout from just behind him shook Adolphus out of his lust for Ward's blood. He glanced over his shoulder to find her watching with wide eyes. Their eyes met, and her expression changed to one of almost supernatural calm.

"He isn't worth it," she said with enough resolve to command an army. "He was never worth it. He'll get what's coming to him."

Again, her expression changed. The barest hint of mischief filled her eyes. It was magnified by her odd costume and the pink that had kissed her cheeks during the chase. She glanced past him to the corner of the stable, which was just visible around the side of the house.

"Good heavens," Lady Rothsay panted, finally catching up to them all. "Isn't this exciting?"

Her question must have prompted Ward into action. With a mighty growl, he pushed at Adolphus. Sense and logic won out over bloodlust, and Adolphus rocked back, allowing Ward to struggle away. The bastard got to his feet, coughing and sputtering, and continued to run toward the stable. Lady Rothsay chased after him.

Eliza lunged forward, grabbing Adolphus's arm and hefting him to his feet. "Hurry," she whispered. "You'll want to be there when he rushes straight into the trap."

Adolphus nodded, then jumped after Ward, Eliza keeping up at his side. There was no need to sprint ahead or to outpace Eliza as they pursued Ward. The man was winded and hampered by Lady Rothsay, who clung to him in an effort to match his pace. All Adolphus and Eliza needed to do was to race fast enough to stay a few steps behind him.

They burst into the stable almost as one. Several of the horses nearest the wide stable door reared back and whinnied at the violent interruption. Ward skittered to a stop, nearly sending Lady Rothsay barreling into a stall door.

She recovered quickly enough to ask, "Where is it? Where is the treasure?"

"Where indeed?" Adolphus growled.

"You won't win this one," Ward called to Adolphus as he dashed deeper into the stable, checking each stall briefly as he went.

"Would they hide a magnificent treasure in a horse stall?" Lady Rothsay asked, still panting and red-faced as she peeked into each stable after Ward moved on.

As they moved deeper into the building, the scent of horse and hay and manure growing stronger, a sound that was as incongruous to the situation as children singing carols would have been hit Adolphus's ears. He frowned in confusion as he shifted directions and marched toward a small door at the back of a side aisle of stalls, but the moment he realized what the grunting and moaning was, his brow shot up.

"That's not—" Eliza started as she kept close to his side, her face bursting into a mask of mirth.

"Get out of my way," Ward demanded, leaping down the aisle and pushing the two of them out of the way. "This prize is mine."

He yanked open the door at the end of the aisle. For one, brief moment, they were all treated to the sight of Miss Ivy, her skirts hiked up, her bodice pulled down low enough to expose her ample, pink-tipped breasts, her head tilted back and her hair loose, as she straddled a man who had to have been the stable master. The stable master leaned back over a huge chest that had been painted gold, half sitting on it, half braced against the wall behind. Miss Ivy rode him like a thoroughbred, which was evidenced by the expression of pure bliss on the man's face.

Of course, the moment the two were discovered, Miss Ivy let out a shriek and the stable master a strangled cry.

Miss Ivy disengaged herself from the stable master, nearly losing her balance and falling to her backside as she did. She whipped around to face her new audience, fumbling to pull her blouse up and cover her breasts, as the stable master flapped about, trying to hide his astounding erection. Adolphus felt awful for interrupting before the man was finished, but there was work to be done.

"Some prize, eh?" Ward rubbed his hands together, a wicked light in his eyes. "Do we all get a go?"

Miss Ivy shrieked in offense, balling her hands into fists—which resulted in her blouse sagging open to expose her enormous breasts once more. She blinked, then yelped again.

"That's him," she said, pointing hard at Ward while looking to Adolphus. "That's him, all right."

"Do you know this woman?" Lady Rothsay asked, her eyes as wide as the moon and her face glowing with merriment. She, too, seemed to appreciate Miss Ivy's bosom.

"I've never seen her in my—" Ward stopped, his mouth gaping wide as realization hit him. "No," he gasped, backpedaling, then turning to scramble toward the door. "No, I don't know her. Get me out of here."

Adolphus caught him before he could retreat more than two steps.

"I'd know his face anywhere," Miss Ivy said, making a more successful effort to close her bodice and cover herself. "Even if his face is a bit banged up. He's the one

119

who trampled poor Bill Jones out in front of The Crown and Scepter."

"I don't know what you're talking about," Ward insisted, struggling against Adolphus but getting nowhere. "I've never heard of the place. I would never patronize a pub down by the docks anyhow."

"So you admit to knowing where Miss Ivy works?" Adolphus said, the triumphant calm of knowing he'd won settling over him.

"I...no. I said no such thing. Let me go. I demand you let me go." Ward continued to push and yank and tug to get away from Adolphus.

"He weren't even served that much at the pub," Miss Ivy went on, resting her hands on her hips. "He come in the place all the time and caused trouble, so Mitch started waterin' down his ale to keep him in line. Didn't stop him from runnin' down poor Bill like he were a dog, though."

"I think that's more than enough to bring him before the judge," Adolphus said with a grin. "And I am inclined to think the judge would be interested in hearing your past of interfering with well-born young maidens as well."

"You can't prove any of it," Ward shouted. "I won't let you—"

He broke off in mid-sentence, jerking away from Adolphus and bursting through the door, back into the rows of stalls.

Adolphus chased after him, Eliza right behind him and Miss Ivy bringing up the rear, but their chase didn't last long. As soon as Ward dashed out into the grey and damp afternoon, he was met by Rufus and Lady Caroline and at least two dozen other house party guests, who had likely come to see the winners of the treasure hunt claim their prize.

"Stop him," Adolphus called out, pointing to Ward. "He's been identified and is under arrest."

Rufus and two other gentlemen captured Ward before he could so much as change direction to get away. Ward struggled for only a moment before giving up and bursting into undignified tears. The pathetic picture he painted was emphasized even more by the ripped dress he wore.

"Miss Ivy identified him, did she?" Rufus asked.

Adolphus nodded once.

Rufus let out a breath of relief. "Thank God that's over." He gestured for the men holding Ward to take him back to the house. "Keep him under lock and key until Gibbon can return him to London."

"Now we can enjoy the party as it was intended to be enjoyed," Lady Caroline added, bursting into a smile. That smile took Adolphus and Eliza in with particular sparkle. Now that his business was concluded, Adolphus found himself in a mood to live up to every expectation the twinkle in Lady Caroline's eyes hinted at.

He reached for Eliza, catching her hand and drawing her close. But before he could do more than grin wolfishly at her, his mind already working on ways to convince her to accept his proposal, one of the guests called out, "What about the prize?"

"Yes, yes," several of the others answered. "Did you find the prize?"

Adolphus glanced back to the stable. Eliza did as well. "I suppose Lady Rothsay won the prize," she said.

"She may need some help returning it to the house," Rufus said, his smile growing.

He nodded toward the stable and the crowd of party guests moved forward with him. Once again, the poor horses in their stalls were surprised and disturbed to be invaded by well-dressed, slightly damp noblemen and women and the noise they made. The din caused by the whispers of expectation was deafening once they were all crammed into the stable. It was almost, but not quite, enough to cover the oddly familiar sounds coming from the room where the treasure chest resided.

"Rufus, you may want to wait—" Adolphus called out, hurrying to the front of the group as Rufus reached the door.

It was too late. In a comical repetition of just minutes early, Rufus threw open the door to the smaller room, revealing the sight of Lady Rothsay, completely naked, riding the stable master in much the same position as Miss Ivy had and with equal intensity. The flurry of chatter from the other house guests stopped abruptly, stretching back through the guests who couldn't actually see into the room but who packed the stable.

Unlike Miss Ivy, however, Lady Rothsay didn't

scream or push away from the stable master. Instead, without breaking her stride, she called over her shoulder in a panting voice, "Just a moment. I'm almost there. Oh!"

Adolphus didn't know whether to gape and sputter in shock or to laugh. He took a large step back, holding out his arms so that the others were forced to move back as well. Rufus shut the door as carefully as he could, leaning his back against it and facing the crowd with a sheepish expression.

"Er, they just need a moment to finish up, then we can carry the treasure back to the house and enjoy it," he said.

"Looks as though Lady Rothsay is already enjoying it," someone in the middle of the crush of people called.

She was met with laughter from the others, but that was drowned out moments later by the unmistakable sound of Lady Rothsay finishing what she'd started with a fantastic cry of, "Yes, dear heavens, yes!"

Adolphus cleared his throat and tugged at his collar as the majority of the people cramming the stable laughed. His discomfort wasn't eased one bit when Eliza took his hand, leaned close, and whispered, "I think Lady Rothsay's definition of a prize is exactly the right one." She leaned even closer. "And I think we should claim our own prize with all due haste."

CHAPTER 10

*E*liza couldn't have imagined events reaching such a satisfying conclusion. In the true spirit of what was becoming the most raucous and scandalous summer house party she had ever known, Lady Rothsay emerged from the room in the stable, dressed in her breeches and doublet once more, to a riotous cheer from the other guests. They carried her and the heavy treasure chest back to the house and the grand parlor.

The chest was opened, revealing bottle after bottle of smuggled, French wine, and the celebration that followed was enough to leave Eliza laughing to the point of tears.

"I dare say that none of the participants in today's activities, or the party in general will be able to remember the myriad scandals that have happened already," she said, clutching her stomach as a stitch formed in her side from all the laughter.

"I dare say they will not be able to show their faces in London again if they do remember," Adolphus muttered.

He watched the madness that followed the wine being opened and glasses being passed around with a frown, but Eliza could tell something about him had changed. She feared she knew what it was, and as much as she delighted in the fact that he'd been triumphant in apprehending Henry for his crimes, she also knew what that meant.

"Will you return to London to hand Henry over to the authorities and to see to his trial?" she asked in a subdued voice, considering the growing volume of the party.

Adolphus dragged his eyes away from the revelers— and those members of the party who lingered around the edges of the room, shocked and, in Lady Malvis's case, disgusted by the debauchery that was unfolding—and stared hard at Eliza. She could see his thoughts whirring behind his expression, could feel the tension pulsing through him.

"It would be jolly if you could stay a bit longer," she said, hating how vulnerable she sounded. She'd only really just found him, after all. She'd never known a man who saw her in such a favorable light before, and for what she was certain were selfish reasons, she wasn't ready to let him go.

He opened his mouth, and she braced herself for a world of excuses and reasons he had to leave her. If he left, she knew she would never see him again. But to her surprise, he shut his mouth, clenching his jaw for a moment, then grasped her hand and led her out of the room.

Eliza's heart sank farther. Surely, the only reason he could have to take her aside was to tell her things that would disappoint her, as she'd always been disappointed in the past.

She was taken utterly by surprise when, the moment they left the grand parlor and its revelries, Adolphus spun her into his arms and closed his mouth over hers in a kiss that left her head spinning and her body throbbing with sudden arousal. He pressed her against the wall, reaching for her leg and lifting her knee up over his hip. The entire, sudden movement left Eliza giddy with excitement and banished the worst of her fears.

"I've never kissed someone in breeches before," he said breathlessly, stroking a hand up her side to cup her breast. "I rather like it."

"I must confess that I have kissed someone in a dress before," Eliza said, glancing mischievously up at him.

Adolphus froze, the fire in his eyes reaching a smoldering height. "You...have?"

Eliza shrugged nonchalantly. "I was locked away in an all-girls school for quite some time." She left her explanation there, leaving it to his imagination to determine how extensive her experiences had been.

He continued to study her with a look of fiendish desire for a moment before swooping in to steal another punishing kiss. It was pure madness for Eliza to enjoy his aggression so much when male aggression had led to so much heartache in the past, but coming from Adolphus, it was a temptation and a challenge, not a demand for submission. He might manhandle her, but she would be as safe as a kitten in his hands, and she would purr just as loudly for him.

She was half convinced that he would tug her breeches down her thighs, spin her around, bend her over one of the decorative tables in the hallway and take her from behind, but as news of the treasure being found reached the other guests, more and more people were marching through the halls.

"Not here," Adolphus growled against her ear, as though he, too, were thinking the same thing. He pushed away from the wall, took her hand, and led her toward the stairs.

Ophelia and Mr. Khan were two of the people rushing down the stairs as Eliza and Adolphus headed up. "Has the treasure been found?" Ophelia asked.

"Yes," Eliza told her, even though Adolphus pulled her on without breaking stride. "And Miss Ivy was found as well. Henry has been taken into custody and Lady Rothsay—oh!" She yelped as Adolphus lifted her into his arms and doubled the speed with which he charged up the stairs.

Eliza only barely caught sight of Ophelia clapping a hand over her mouth to hide her laughter as Adolphus marched around the corner onto the upstairs hall. He moved with purpose, managing the increasingly loose folds of his costume dress's skirt, toward his bedroom.

The moment he reached the room, practically kicking the door in, and set Eliza on her feet once more, he tore at the silly dress. Its ties had already come loose in back and the whole thing fell away like a cobweb swatted out of a corner. But he didn't stop there. He went to work straight away on the buttons of his coat and waistcoat, which he hadn't had a chance to remove before the play.

"Oh, dear, you do look serious," Eliza said, backing playfully away from him toward the bed. "Or perhaps this is a lesson on how one removes a coat and breeches?" She arched an eyebrow, then glanced down at her costume.

She reached for the buttons of her doublet, but Adolphus stopped her with a loud, "Don't."

Eliza was so startled—and aroused by the dark look of command he sent her—that she dropped her hands instantly to her sides.

"I want to remove those myself," Adolphus went on, tossing his coat and waistcoat aside.

He continued his own process of undressing by yanking loose his cravat and throwing it to the floor, then tugging his shirt out of his breeches and over his head with such force that a button popped off. The sound of it hitting the wall then bouncing on the floor should not have turned Eliza's cunny to molten need, but it did.

Or perhaps it was the sight of Adolphus's broad, powerful chest. His muscles rippled as he bent to pull off his boots. Every inch of him was pure masculinity, even the abrasions on his knuckles and the bruise forming on the side of his face from where he and Henry had brawled. It was pure madness to be enticed by those signs of aggression instead of frightened by them, but they were simply more symbols of the ferocity with which Adolphus would protect her.

By the time he straightened and worked open the front of his breeches, staring at her with a look of outrageous lust as he did, Eliza was so hot under her doublet and breeches that she ached to be freed from them. When he let the falls of his breeches go, pushing the restrictive garment down over his hips so that his thick cock leapt straight up, she was so overcome that she sat heavily on the side of the bed.

"This is no time for rest," Adolphus said, stepping out of his breeches and kicking them aside. "Rest is the very last thing I have in mind for you."

"Oh?" she asked, her voice trembling.

He stalked toward her, so intimidating when he reached her that she flopped to her back on the bed. He planted his hands on either side of her and leaned close to say, "You have played your last game with me, Lady Elizabeth Towers." His use of her full name caused her sex to squeeze and ache to be filled. "You will marry me."

Her heart slammed against her ribs. For a moment she couldn't breathe. The only answer she could give was a long, sensual sigh.

Apparently, that wasn't good enough for him. He

rocked back, taking hold of her half-soaked shoes and prying them off her feet. Once they were gone, he undid the buttons of her breeches and tugged them from her legs in one, smooth motion. The sudden swirl of cool air around her legs and hips did nothing to return her powers of speech, though. Neither did the way he took hold of her ankles and wrenched them apart, forcing her to bend her knees and open her legs wide to him. If the feeling of air against her legs left her breathless, the sudden coolness against her gaping sex left her groaning.

"You will marry me," Adolphus repeated, sliding one hand down her thigh and stroking his fingers across her wet entrance, "or I will never put my cock inside of you and stretch you until you weep with pleasure ever again."

Eliza yelped in protest, then arched her hips against his teasing hand. "You're bluffing," she panted. "You want me as much as I want you."

He hesitated, proving that she was absolutely correct. His shoulders sagged for half a second before a renewed grin of power and provocation danced across his lips. "Of course, I want you," he said, circling his fingers around her clitoris and causing the most delicious sensations within her before sinking two fingers deep into her aching folds. "But I have more experience with self-denial. I can hold out longer than you."

She wanted to argue his point, but his hands had worked their magic on her. She could feel the coil of pleasure that would burst into orgasm squeezing tighter and tighter inside of her. She was so close she closed her eyes, ready to feel the whole thing intensely. But he drew his hand away, leaving her frustrated and desperate.

"No," she groaned as he stood straight, taking a half step back from the bed. To make things worse, he took hold of himself and stroked, a look of wicked defiance in his eyes. "No," she gasped even louder. "That's not fair."

"I can still enjoy myself without sinking deep into you," he said, his voice little more than an impassioned rumble.

"You wouldn't dare," she said, glaring at him and sitting up. She kept her legs apart as she did. More than that, she rushed through the buttons of her doublet, pulling it open, then scrambling to undo the ties of her stays. She'd kept her stays and chemise on while changing into the silly costume, but now she wished she hadn't.

It was next to impossible to force her fingers to work or to still the wild pounding of her heart as he stroked himself harder. He was a villain if he thought he could bring himself to completion without treating her to the joy of feeling him inside of her. The only weapon she had to beat him at his own game was to show him what he was missing.

At last, she struggled out of the doublet and her stays and chemise, then arched her back to show him just how sensual she could be. She went beyond that, drawing on every trick she had to make him lose control, and grasped one of her breasts. A surge of victory pulsed through her as his gaze dropped hungrily to watch what her hand was doing. She took advantage of the moment and slipped her hand slowly down over her belly.

"Perhaps I should show you some of the things I practiced with my schoolmates," she said, biting her lip and sending him the most wicked look she could as her fingers delved into her curls. His imagination would decide what she meant and whether it was the truth or a clever lie.

It was exactly the trigger he needed. With a muttered oath, he let go of himself and surged onto the bed with her. He brought his hips to hers and jerked inside of her without teasing or niceties. She cried out in shock and pleasure and delight as he filled and stretched her. But for once, she didn't curse herself for being wanton or embrace deep feelings of shame at her body's response. He was hers, and the way he claimed her, like a warrior claiming his prize, was exactly the way things should be.

His thrusts were hard and purposeful. There would be no more teasing or drawing their mating out. She was already hovering on the brinks, and when he tensed, jerking desperately into her as he came, she burst into orgasm herself. The sensation of milking him for all he was worth as he spilled his seed within her was so shattering that her pleasure went on and on. She'd never known completion so wonderful before and she didn't want it to ever end.

All beautiful things come to an end, though. Too soon, the surging tide of passion began to ebb, and Adolphus sank to her side with a deep, satisfied groan. But then he did something else, something Eliza never would have expected.

He laughed.

The sound was a revelation, filling her with energy as she rolled to her side and propped herself on one arm to gaze down at him. Everything about him was transformed by the sound of his laughter, by the broad smile that relaxed his face in a way she'd never seen before. His whole body shook, filling her with joy.

"Am I that funny?" she asked, giggling herself.

"No," he said, shaking his head and sighing, then laughing all over again. "I only just realized."

"What have you realized?" Her own laughter grew more and more uncontrollable as he failed to bring himself into line.

He glanced up at her, resting a hand on the side of her face. "I've realized that I love you. I really and truly love you. Though it's madness to think how. We hardly know each other."

"We know each other better than most couples ever do," she said, pushing herself so that she sat straddling his hips. She stroked her hands over his damp chest, playing with his nipples. "Didn't you have a question to ask me?" she asked, one eyebrow raised.

His eyes widened, as though he couldn't believe she was asking such a thing in that moment. Then his expression settled into as much seriousness as the laughter that remained in his eyes would allow. "Will you marry me?" he asked.

"Why do you want to marry me?" she fired back at him, grinning with all her might because she knew that this time, he would come up with the right answer.

"Because you're mine," he said, a richer note in his voice. "Because I'm yours. Because I want to protect you and give you a happy life. Because you deserve to be treated like the goddess you are." He paused, understanding widening the smile he wore. "And because I love you," he finished.

Eliza's heart had never been lighter. She leaned forward, slanting her mouth over his and kissing him with far more power than a woman was supposed to kiss a man. He responded readily, circling his hands around her backside and squeezing. It was all the sign Eliza needed to know that they wouldn't be leaving his room, or his bed, for quite some time to come. She looked forward to every second of it, guilt-free.

"Yes," she said at last, pulling back just a bit, so that her nose was only inches from his. "If you love me, of course I'll marry you. Nothing in the entire world would make me happier, because I love you with my whole heart."

EPILOGUE

*O*phelia held her breath and inserted the key that she still wore on a ribbon around her neck into the lock on the chest that had contained the prize at the end of the treasure hunt. Every one of the party guests who had taken part in the drunken revelry at the end of the hunt—and it was by no means all of Caro's guests—were still sleeping off the effects of the prize. That meant Ophelia had the perfect opportunity to sneak into the grand parlor to see whether the prize chest had something to do with her key.

Of course, it didn't. The key she'd found was much too small for the chest's lock, but she had hoped there was some sort of secret compartment within the chest that the key could unlock. She was disappointed yet again and stood with a sigh.

"Good heavens. What was that for?"

Ophelia whirled around with a start, her heart

pounding against her ribs, to find Mr. Saif Khan standing only a few yards away, watching her.

"I was...that is to say...I was just...."

"You don't need to explain to me," Mr. Khan said, walking slowly up to her side. "We did our best to win the prize for ourselves, but without luck."

"It's not that," Ophelia said, lowering her eyes. Mr. Khan was so deliciously handsome that she found it impossible to look at him without giving every one of her tender feelings for the exotic man away in an instant.

"Are you sad that your friend has left, then?" he asked, stepping closer.

Ophelia dared herself to look at him. Others might have been taken aback because he was Indian, but he had the kindest eyes of anyone she'd ever know. The exotic additions to his otherwise ordinary clothing—the silk waistcoat with its Indian print and the ruby pin that she had come to think of as a tiger's eyes in his cravat—thrilled her. And that was before she even began to try to describe the way his accent tickled her toes, and other places.

With a start, she remembered he'd asked a question. "I haven't had time to be sad. Eliza only left this morning," she said. "She and Mr. Gibbon will be married in London, just as soon as they deposit Mr. Ward at Newgate Prison."

"Yes, what a curious and unpleasant business," Mr. Khan answered, though the way he watched her seemed to say that everything was magnificently pleasant. "Her family won't mind if she is married without them?"

"Her family hasn't minded about much in Eliza's life thus far," Ophelia confessed.

"And you?" he asked on.

Ophelia blinked. "Me?"

"Does your family mind about you?"

She blinked again, going hot from head to toe. "My father only minds that I find a suitable husband. Aunt Millicent is here to make certain I do."

"What does your father consider suitable?" He seemed far more curious about the answer than Ophelia dared to hope for.

She shrugged. "A fortune, I suppose. And lofty connections."

"I see." Mr. Khan's smile widened. "Is that why you seemed so disappointed, then? Have you not set your heart on any of the wealthy, lofty gentlemen at the party?"

Heat blossomed on Ophelia's cheeks. How could she explain to him that the only man she had found even remotely attractive was one her father would never approve of?

She grasped the key around her neck. "It's this key," she said, counting her statement as a half-truth. "I have been searching for what it might unlock for a fortnight now."

"May I see?" he said, stepping forward.

Ophelia held her breath as he handled the key, letting

it rest in his palm as the back of his hand came tantalizingly close to brushing her breasts. Every wicked feeling that she wasn't supposed to have but had never had any luck in suppressing rushed to the fore.

At last, Mr. Khan glanced up at her, his eyes seeming to sparkle with heat and mischief, like the haze she had read about during the Indian monsoon.

"You are in luck, Lady Ophelia," he said. "I know what this key belongs to."

I HOPE YOU HAVE ENJOYED ELIZA AND ADOLPHUS'S story! I'm so happy that the two of them got their happily ever after! And what about Ophelia and Saif? Is it possible for the two of them to be together? And what on earth does Ophelia's key unlock? Find out in the next When the Wallflowers were Wicked book, *The Charming Jezebel*!

IF YOU ENJOYED THIS BOOK AND WOULD LIKE TO HEAR more from me, please sign up for my newsletter! When you sign up, you'll get a free, full-length novella, *A Passionate Deception*. Victorian identity theft has never been so exciting in this story of hope, tricks, and starting over. Part of my *West Meets East* series, *A Passionate Deception* can be read as a stand-alone. Pick up your free copy today by signing up to receive my newsletter (which I only send out when I have a new release)!

Sign up here: http://eepurl.com/cbaVMH

Click here for a complete list of other works by Merry Farmer.

ABOUT THE AUTHOR

I hope you have enjoyed *The Playful Wanton*. If you'd like to be the first to learn about when new books in the series come out and more, please sign up for my newsletter here: http://eepurl.com/cbaVMH And remember, Read it, Review it, Share it! For a complete list of works by Merry Farmer with links, please visit http://wp.me/P5ttjb-14F.

Merry Farmer is an award-winning novelist who lives in suburban Philadelphia with her cats, Torpedo, her grumpy old man, and Justine, her hyperactive new baby. She has been writing since she was ten years old and realized one day that she didn't have to wait for the teacher to assign a creative writing project to write something. It was the best day of her life. She then went on to earn not one but two degrees in History so that she would always have something to write about. Her books have reached the Top 100 at Amazon, iBooks, and Barnes & Noble, and have been named finalists in the prestigious RONE and Rom Com Reader's Crown awards.

ACKNOWLEDGMENTS

I owe a huge debt of gratitude to my awesome beta-readers, Caroline Lee and Jolene Stewart, for their suggestions and advice. And double thanks to Julie Tague, for being a truly excellent editor and assistant! Thanks also to the members of the Historical Harlots Facebook Group, who provide me with all sorts of inspiration!

Click here for a complete list of other works by Merry Farmer.

CPSIA information can be obtained
at www.ICGtesting.com
Printed in the USA
LVHW080508060420
652341LV00008B/581

9 781687 478078